THE POWER OF A NAME

Mr. Melas shrugged. "Everything in Everidge is the Winchesters'. They own the mills and the bank and half the houses the people live in. You don't get elected unless they say so. You think the cops would do anything the Winchesters didn't like? Chris, you got to understand, people around here don't like your family. And now they're going to try to bust the union and cut wages."

"Mr. Melas, why am I getting the blame? It doesn't have anything to do with me."

"Your name's Winchester, Chris. That'll be enough for most people around here..."

Other Avon Flare Books by
James Lincoln Collier

OUTSIDE LOOKING IN

the Winchesters

JAMES LINCOLN COLLIER

AN AVON FLARE BOOK

AVON BOOKS
A division of
The Hearst Corporation
1350 Avenue of the Americas
New York, New York 10019

Copyright © 1988 by James Lincoln Collier
Published by arrangement with Macmillan Publishing Company
Library of Congress Catalog Card Number: 88-5364
ISBN: 0-380-70808-6
RL: 4.9

First Avon Flare Printing: November 1989

AVON FLARE TRADEMARK REG. U.S. PAT. OFF. AND IN OTHER COUNTRIES, MARCA REGISTRADA, HECHO EN CANADA

Printed in Canada

UNV   10 9 8 7 6 5 4 3

For Marjory

CHAPTER 1

We were walking along the bluestone driveway under the branches of the sugar maples way up above, when we heard the sound of voices somewhere over by the pond. It was the kind of shouting and laughing that kids do when they're fooling around in the water. We were screened off from the pond by the pine trees around the end of it.

"What's that?" my cousin Ernest said. We never called him Ernie, always Ernest. Ernie was too low class. The Winchesters didn't allow anyone in the family to be called by nicknames. Except me. They called me Chris, not Christopher.

"It sounds like somebody's in the pond," I said.

"They shouldn't be," Ernest said. "Let's get them out of there."

Ernest liked to fight. The funny thing about that was that he went to prep school, where he had to say sir to the teachers and wear a jacket and tie to class every day, and I went to public school where most of the kids didn't even own a necktie and wouldn't say sir to anybody unless you held a gun on them. But Ernest was the

1

one who liked to fight. He played blocking back on his prep school football team and defense on the hockey team and he liked knocking people down.

I wasn't so much on fighting. I'd do it if I had to, so as not to be chicken, but I didn't get any thrill out of it. "It's a hot day," I said. "They just want to cool off."

"They have the town pool." He frowned and brushed his hair back out of his eyes. Most of the Winchesters had blond hair, but my hair was dark brown, which I got from my mother.

"Yeah, but the town pool is usually pretty crowded." It was beautiful under the arch of the sugar maples. Our great-grandfather had planted them a long time ago, when he built the big house where Ernest lived, so that the driveway was always cool and shaded, with bits and patches of sun coming through here and there.

"What right have they got to complain?" Ernest said. "We gave the town that pool."

The town pool was twenty years old. A lot of the tiles had fallen off, and the fence around it was bent and rusty. Besides, it was all the way down at one end of the town park, and there were always trucks grinding by, sending off a lot of exhaust. "They don't like it. There's too much traffic. Besides, on a day like this it'll be jammed."

Ernest was still frowning. "What do they want for nothing? We paid for the pool."

"I thought the mills paid for it."

"It's the same thing." He looked at me. "Come on. Let's get them out of there."

"They're not doing any harm."

2

"They'll leave soda cans around. Besides, if we let some of them come, the next thing you know half the town will be up here swimming all summer long. Then you'll have a mess—people leaving their garbage around and throwing stuff in the water and playing radios loud. Besides, Dad says that if somebody drowns we're responsible."

I knew that Ernest was right. If you let people from the town come up to the estate and use the place, they'd take it over. Still, it was hard to see why the whole town should be jammed into one pool and we should have a whole pond five times as big for ourselves.

"Come on, let's go," Ernest said.

"Maybe we should get Durham." Durham was the groundskeeper. You always called servants by their last names. I didn't know why. Durham was black and had been in Viet Nam and had a scar on his face from a fragmentation bomb.

Ernest looked at me. "What are you, Chris—chicken?"

"No, I'm not chicken." It wasn't that—it wasn't that at all. The reason why I was arguing was because the kids in the pond were liable to be somebody I knew at school. They might be in my class when school started or on the baseball team with me. I'd been going to that school from first grade, and I'd had some of the same kids with me all the way through eighth grade. I sure didn't want to have to tell them to get out of the pond.

"Come on. Let's go," Ernest said. He turned off the bluestone driveway toward the pond. My great-grandfather had put in the pond, too. There had been a

3

kind of swampy place there with a spring underneath. He'd hired a gang of men to dig it out. He'd had pines planted in a semicircle at the west end, the end away from the big house. Between the house and the pond there was nothing but lawn, so from what they called the ballroom, on the west side of the house, you could see the water. It was beautiful when the sun set through the pines and turned the water orange; it was beautiful in winter with a sheet of snow stretching fifty yards from the house down to the pond, covered with ice. It was beautiful, too, to skate on the pond. Durham always cleared the ice with the snow blower and then watered it, so that it was always slick and fast. We would skate there, Ernest and me and his sister, Anne, and their friends—they usually brought friends home from prep school for vacations. Toward the end of the afternoon, when the sun was going down, the windows of the big house would be squares of orange, so bright you could hardly look at them.

Ernest was running toward the pine trees. He looked back. "Come on, Chris," he shouted.

Ernest always tried to get me to do what he wanted me to. He didn't know he did that, but he did. Someday he was going to be boss of a huge business worth millions and millions—the family had never let it out how much—and he was already getting into the habit of giving orders. It didn't bother me that he did that. He was *supposed* to get in the habit of giving orders. In fact, I kind of admired him for it. I wasn't much on giving orders myself, and I wasn't sure that I could ever learn. But Ernest was my cousin and he was my friend, and so

I would never let him boss me around too much. Sometimes I would do what he wanted, and sometimes I wouldn't. It all depended.

But this time I was stuck. He thought he had a right to chase these kids out of the pond. In fact, he thought it was his duty to do it. He thought if he didn't do it, he would be chicken. He thought that if we got Durham, instead of kicking these kids out ourselves, that would be chicken, too. Ernest would never understand if I didn't help him. Anyway, the best thing would be if I went with him to see if I could settle it some way. So I raced after him through the mowed field and caught up with him just as he was going into the pines. I loved going into the pines, feeling the needles soft underfoot and smelling that sweetish pine smell, which came up strong on a hot day like this. We jogged on through the pines and came out onto the bank of the pond.

There were three kids in the water, splashing around and shouting. Their bikes were lying among the pines on the pine needles, along with their clothes and a couple of soda cans they'd dropped. We stood on the bank looking out at the kids. They were splashing each other, and I couldn't see who they were.

"Hey," Ernest shouted. "You're not supposed to swim here."

The kids stopped splashing, and now I could see who they were. One of them was Benny Briggs. The other two were guys he hung around with. I didn't know their names for sure, but one of them had a French-Canadian name, like Goffere or something. I knew Benny Briggs, all right. He was a year ahead of me in school and had been on the junior-high-school baseball team with me the year before, when he was in eighth grade and I was in seventh. He was going to Everidge High already, and maybe I'd be on the baseball team with him again.

"You're not supposed to swim here," Ernest shouted again.

They didn't get out, but stayed there, treading water. "Don't give me any of that," Briggs shouted. "This pond doesn't belong to you." Benny was a kind of tall, gangly kid with black hair and a long face. He played shortstop. He was pretty good.

"Yes, it does," Ernest shouted. "It's ours. You can't swim in it."

Then Briggs recognized me. "Hey, Winchester, are you trying to tell me this lake belongs to this guy?"

"It belongs to his family," I said.

"Come off it, Winchester," Briggs said, still treading water. "This lake doesn't belong to anybody."

"It sure does," Ernest said. "It belongs to us. You guys get out."

Ernest didn't understand what was going on in Benny's mind, but I did. Benny's folks worked for the Winchester Mills. I didn't know exactly what they did, but it was on an assembly line putting together condensers, or spray-painting steam valves or something. They weren't poor, but they weren't rich, either, and got laid off here and there. They probably never could afford a new car, but always got one three or four years old. They couldn't afford to own a motorboat, and they lived on the second floor of one of the old wooden houses on a back street in town. For fun they watched

TV and, on hot summer nights, sat in the backyard of a friend who had a backyard and drank beer and ate potato salad and hot dogs. Sure, they probably had as good a time as most people, except for worrying about getting laid off. I knew all about that, because a lot of the kids from school lived like that. In fact, my girlfriend, Marie Scalzo, lived like that, except her dad didn't work for the Winchester Mills, but ran a little store.

She and her sister shared a room, and her older brother, Frankie, had a bed in the little storeroom behind the store.

Most of these people didn't have any real idea of what it was like to be rich. Benny Briggs just couldn't understand that anybody could own a whole pond. Something like a pond would just be *there*, and wouldn't belong to anybody any more than the Atlantic Ocean belonged to anybody. Oh, he knew he wasn't supposed to swim in it. For people like the Briggses, there were a lot of things they weren't supposed to do. But they did them anyway, if they figured they could get away with it.

I knew about that, too, because when I was little and first came to live in the gatehouse on the Winchester estate, I was scared of doing nearly everything. I figured I wasn't allowed to ride my bike on the driveway or play ball on the grass, and I wouldn't go into the big house unless somebody told me to, and wouldn't go in by the front door, either, but always went in through the laundry room.

I'd got over a lot of that from hanging around with

Ernest, who could do what he pleased and go wherever he wanted. He rode his bike on the driveway and played ball on the grass, and I went along with him. But I still wouldn't go into the big house unless I had a reason for it, and I still always went in through the laundry room, unless it was Christmas or Thanksgiving and I went up with Mom and the twins, all dressed up in a suit and a tie. Then we went in through the front door.

So I knew how Benny Briggs felt. But Ernest didn't. He didn't have any idea of what Benny Briggs was like at all. Ernest knew that some people had more money than other people, but he couldn't imagine what it was really like. He couldn't imagine that some kids never had their own room, but had to share with brothers and sisters. He couldn't imagine that some kids had never been in a powerboat or gone water skiing. So it wasn't just meanness that made him want to get Benny and the other guys out of the pond. He couldn't imagine that they didn't have a decent place to swim.

"Listen," Ernest shouted. "You guys better get out of there."

Briggs flopped over and began to do a backstroke. "Who's going to make us?" he said. He turned his head and sucked up some water and spurted it in the air.

There were three of them and they were older than us, but I knew that wouldn't stop Ernest from going after them. "I'm giving you a last chance," he shouted.

The other two guys weren't swimming, but were still treading water. "Hey, Benny," the French-Canadian kid said. "Maybe we better get out of here."

"What for? This kid doesn't own this lake."

"I told you, it belongs to my family," Ernest said. He figured he was in the right and they were wrong, and he was getting sore. He was getting ready to go after them.

"Up yours," Benny said. He spurted some more water in the air.

Suddenly Ernest pulled his T-shirt over his head and flung it on the ground. Then he kicked off his running shoes and began tearing off his socks.

"Ernest," I said. "Take it easy a little. You can't fight them all."

He looked at me. "You're going to help me, aren't you?"

Out in the water Benny Briggs had stopped floating around and was treading water with the other guys, watching to see what we were going to do. I knew that if Ernest went in the water after them, I'd have to go with him. "Ernest, calm down a minute," I said.

He gave me another look and began taking off his jeans. "Are you coming with me or not?"

"Ernest—"

"Are you coming, Chris?"

I looked out at Benny Briggs. Ernest would go for him first, I knew. "Sure, I'm coming." I began to kick off my shoes and strip off my T-shirt. The best thing I could do would be to let Ernest fight Benny and see if I could keep the other guys out of it while they fought. My heart was beating pretty fast. The last time I'd been in a real fight was with Ernest. He'd checked me too hard when we were playing hockey and I lost my temper and tackled him, and we'd rolled around on the ice for a while trying to slug each other until Durham came down and broke it up. I knew I could fight if I had to, but there were three of them against two. I felt scared, all right, but I figured you were bound to be scared if you were going into a fight.

Ernest had got his clothes off. "Hurry up, Chris."

One of the guys in the water said, "Benny, maybe we better get out of here."

"No way," Briggs said. "I'm not scared of these guys."

I slipped out of my jeans and stood on the bank, ready to go. "Let's go," Ernest said.

Then there came a low, rough shout. I turned and looked. Durham was standing on the lawn by the side of the pond that faced the house. He had Duchess, the big Doberman, on a leash. Duchess was stretched out at the end of the leash. If Durham let her go she'd tear into the water after those guys and chop them up. "You people get outta there," Durham shouted. "And you stay the hell outta there."

But already Briggs and his friends were swimming as fast as they could toward the other end of the pond where their bikes lay among the pine trees.

CHAPTER 2

My mother had a genealogy of the Winchester family that showed all of our ancestors going way back. We could trace some branches of the family back to the 1500s. There were lots of famous people in our genealogy—a governor, two senators, a famous general in the Revolution, a lot of people who fought in the Civil War, and some others. I never could keep them all straight. But my mother said, "Your dad always said that most of the people in the genealogy were just plain people—farmers and fishermen and storekeepers who worked hard all their lives and tried to do right by their families. Only a few of them back there were important. The Winchesters are always going on about General Markham and Governor Winchester, but mostly they come from plain people, just like everybody else. Your dad always made a point of that."

I guess he was right, for the Winchester money didn't go all that far back. The business was started by my great-great-grandfather. He was born in 1855, before the Civil War. There was a portrait of him, big as a

11

window, hanging in the dining room in the big house. He had on a dark suit and a white shirt, and he looked very fierce. It was one of those pictures where the eyes follow you around the room—no matter where you went, he always looked at you. He used to scare the daylights out of me when I was little. We would go up there for Thanksgiving or Christmas, when they had a big family dinner for all the cousins—thirty or forty people maybe, three turkeys, plum pudding from England, thousands of dollars worth of glassware and silver gleaming so bright the table sparkled. But the whole time I was there I had the idea that that old man was staring at me, just staring and staring, waiting for me to make a mistake in my manners so he could jump out of that picture and start shaking me by the collar.

His name was Amos Winchester. He was some kind of a cloth salesman, traveling around Massachusetts. One time he ran into this crazy inventor who'd figured out an improved safety valve for steam engines. Amos Winchester made an agreement with him. He got some people to back him, and he set up a factory to make this improved safety valve. It was a huge success. Steam engines were coming along big at that time, because the railroads were expanding all over the United States, steam engines were taking over from water power in factories, ships were switching to steam from sail. In the end it turned out that the inventor, who didn't know anything about business, had signed all the rights to the valve over to my great-great-grandfather. He ended up owning the whole thing.

My great-great-grandfather expanded into making

steam gauges, and then various kinds of steam pipe, and finally whole steam engines. By the time he died, in 1921, he had a big factory going and had made himself rich. He was the one who bought the land for the Winchester estate and built the first part of the big house, using a kind of stone that was quarried right around Everidge. The house was square, then: four rooms downstairs, four rooms upstairs, and some little rooms on the third floor for the servants and storage.

After he died his son, my great-grandfather Edward, took over the mill and the house and everything. Automobiles were coming along then. He expanded into carburetors, and then electrical parts for cars—generators and so forth. He made even more money and expanded the mill and added a wing to the house with a ballroom in it, and guest rooms upstairs.

His oldest son turned out to be a black sheep. He ran off to live in Paris and be a writer and a Bohemian, and spent all of his life trying to get money out of the family. So the mills and the house went to the second son, who was my grandfather. He was called Ernest, but nobody in the family ever called him anything but Skipper. That was because he loved boats and had twelve-metres and even raced one in the America's Cup trials once. He had a big yacht that he kept down in Rhode Island, even though by now he lived in Switzerland, where the taxes were lower.

My grandfather put the rear wing on the house, with a new kitchen and flower room my grandmother wanted when she married him. He was the boss of the whole thing when the Depression came, and the townspeople always blamed him for a lot of what happened. When business went bad at that time, my grandfather shut the mill and laid off nearly everybody. The old people in Everidge remembered those days and would talk about them. They remembered eating nothing but potatoes for dinner night after night, and patching the holes in their shoes with cardboard because they couldn't afford to buy new ones. My grandfather said that he had to lay everybody off to save the business, and it's true that when times got better he hired them all back again. But the old people said he didn't have to do it, he could have kept the business going if he'd been willing to risk his own money in it.

My dad was born in 1945. He was the oldest son, and by rights he would have become head of the family. But my dad was different from most of the Winchesters—different from most people. When he got out of college he told Skipper that he didn't want to spend his life sitting in that fancy office down at the Winchester Mills, trying to figure out ways to make more money. According to Mom, he said he knew what you had to do to people sometimes when you ran a business. He said he didn't blame old Amos Winchester for cheating that inventor, and he didn't blame Skipper for shutting down the mills during the Depression. He said he understood that if you were in business, sometimes you had to do these things. But he didn't want to do them himself. So when he graduated from Harvard, where the Winchesters always went, he joined the Peace Corps. His younger brother, my uncle Foster, took over the Winchester Mills, and instead of me living up there

14

in the big house and looking forward to being rich, Ernest got it.

The day after Ernest and I almost got into a fight with those guys at the pond, Uncle Foster called us in to his office to give us a talking-to. Of course he had an office down at the mills, where he went most days. I'd been there a couple of times when I'd had to take papers down to him. That office was bigger than most people's living rooms. It had a fireplace and a window looking out on the mills, antique furniture, and a huge Oriental carpet that covered most of the floor and cost fifty thousand dollars.

But he also had an office in the house. For example, Mom kept all her papers and junk in a little cardboard file. When she had to pay the bills or figure out her taxes, she dumped the papers out on the old oak table in the kitchen that we ate on, and sat there with her cup of tea, adding and subtracting—mostly subtracting, she usually said.

But Uncle Foster had a whole lot more than his taxes to worry about. He was on the board of trustees of two colleges; he was on the board of directors of three or four charities, including the Winchester Foundation, which gave money for research into heart disease; he was on the board of the Everidge Bank, which the Winchesters pretty much owned; he was on the boards of a couple of other big companies. Running a rich family was like running a business. Mom had the job of taking care of the bills and paying the servants and such. She said that managing the house alone was like running a small hotel.

The office was in a back corner of the house, at the side away from the pond. It had been Skipper's office before it was Uncle Foster's, and my great-grandfather's before him. Ernest and I went along the hall from the small dining room. I felt pretty nervous. "What's he going to do to us?" I asked.

"I don't care," Ernest said. "We didn't do anything wrong. I'm going to argue with him." What worried me most was that Uncle Foster would want to know who those kids in the pond were. We got to the office door and knocked. He told us to come in.

There were a lot of books along the walls and pictures of various famous ships that Skipper had had painted, an old barometer that came from some ship the Winchesters had owned, and a couple of easy chairs. Uncle Foster sat behind his desk—an old teakwood desk that had been bought by my great-grandfather when he put in the office. Uncle Foster liked to sit leaning back with his feet up on his wastebasket. He was reading some papers. Ernest flopped down in one of the easy chairs, but I didn't dare. I stood there by the door, looking out the window. The crushed stone driveway swung around behind the house here to get to the stable, where they kept the riding horses, and the old carriage house, where the cars were garaged. They had a Porsche, a Mercedes, a big Lincoln limo, a four-wheel-drive Jeep for emergencies in the winter, and a Datsun pickup for Durham to use around the place.

Durham was out there now, polishing the Lincoln limo in the sun. He went over it every morning, so there

16

would never be a speck of dirt on it. He once told me, "Chris, you never know when they'll want it. Your uncle Foster, he'll get on the house phone and tell me to shoot into Logan Airport to pick up Senator Whosis or Secretary Whatzis. I don't hardly have no time to put on my uniform, I can't fool around cleaning no car." The stable boy did the Mercedes and the Porsche, but Durham took a lot of pride in the limo, and wouldn't let anybody else touch it. It was almost like he thought he owned it.

Finally Uncle Foster put the papers down and swiveled around in his chair to face us. "Ernest, sit up straight. You can sit down, Chris." I sat down in the other easy chair. Uncle Foster looked at us for a minute. Then he said, "What was it all about, boys?"

Ernest was sitting up straight. "Those guys shouldn't have been in the pond. We were going to kick them out, only Durham came with Duchess."

"There were three of them, Durham told me."

"I wasn't scared of them," Ernest said. "We'd have beat them if Durham hadn't come."

Uncle Foster didn't pay any attention to that, but looked at me. "Do you know who they were, Chris?"

I knew he was bound to catch me if I lied. I began to blush. "I don't think they would have hurt anything," I said.

"I didn't ask that," he said.

Ernest looked at me. "That one guy knew you."

I went on blushing, because they knew I was thinking about lying.

"I know who one of them is, Uncle Foster. Benny

17

Briggs. He's a year ahead of me in school."

"Benny Briggs?" He took a pen out of the fancy pen holder on his desk and made a note on a yellow pad. "What do you know about him, Chris?"

"Well, I don't know him too well, Uncle Foster. We were on the baseball team when he was in eighth grade and I was in seventh. He played shortstop."

"Shortstop? I played shortstop in school. Is he any good?"

"Pretty good," I said. "He has a real good arm."

"Really good," Uncle Foster said.

I wasn't doing anything right. "Really good," I said.

"You don't want to start picking up that kind of language from these fellows," he said.

I thought, if I wasn't supposed to pick up that kind of language, maybe I ought to go to prep school where I'd meet different fellows. "Yes, sir."

"Where does he live, this Briggs boy?"

I hated being grilled about it. I didn't want to tell on Benny, but I hated lying. There wasn't much harm in telling Uncle Foster where Benny lived, because he could find out easily enough. "Up on Granite Street. I think, anyway. Somewhere up there."

"What about the other two?"

I was safe there, because I really didn't know who they were, I only *thought* I knew who one of them was. "I don't know them," I said. "Friends of Benny's, I guess."

Uncle Foster stared at me. "You sure you don't know them, Chris?"

18

Of course I wasn't sure. I hoped I wou'
again. "I might have seen them around o
but I don't know their names."

"Would you be able to identify them if I decia
anything about it?"

I sure didn't want to have anything to do with that.
"I'm not—"

"I could," Ernest said. "I could identify them, all
right."

"It might not be worth pursuing," Uncle Foster said.
Then he swiveled his chair around, put his feet on the
wastebasket, and leaned back, staring out the window.
I took a look out. Durham was going over the uphol-
stery with a little vacuum cleaner that plugged into the
cigarette lighter. I knew about it, because I'd helped
him clean the limo a few times. "But I'm bringing it up
because there may be more to it than it seems." He
went on looking out the window. "I don't want to say
too much at this point, but I think I'd better tell you
something about it, because you may be facing a lot of
animosity in town. Especially you, Chris. People will be
saying things to you, and you'll have to learn how to
handle it better than you boys did yesterday."

"It's the strike, isn't it, Dad?" Ernest said. "There's
going to be a strike."

Uncle Foster took his feet off the wastebasket and
swung around to look at us. "I don't know how much
you know about this, Chris, but Ernest knows something. We've had some problems with foreign competition over the past few years. Foreign manufacturers can

e some things cheaper than we can. Especially in
e electronics area. Our electronics division has been
osing money recently. Cheaper labor abroad is the reason, mostly. In some countries they can pay their workers a third or a quarter of what American workers have
to be paid. It doesn't take much calculating to see what
that means. We think we'll be able to get around it in
the end, but it's going to take some doing. We're going
to have to make some economies, and about the only
place we can reduce expenses in any substantial way is
by cutting wages. Our union contract is coming up
soon, and we're going to ask our people to take a cut. If
we don't, we'll go on losing money, and we can only
bleed so long. Eventually we'd have to close down the
electronics division. That would throw three thousand
people out of work here. That's a quarter of the families
in town."

He paused and gave us a long look. "Word's already
going around about it, boys. They don't like it. There's
going to be a lot of animosity. The chances of a strike
are good. Maybe other kinds of trouble."

"What kind of trouble?" Ernest said. I could see he
had a liking for the idea of trouble.

Uncle Foster shrugged. "There's no way of knowing.
But once you get a strike, you get violence. The only
thing we can hope for is that the majority of people will
see our point. They have to understand that if we can't
compete with foreign competition we'll go out of business. It's as simple as that."

I didn't want to say anything. What was it going to
be like at school for me if half the town was mad at the

Winchesters? Ernest said, "Why couldn't they under-stand that?"

"A lot of them will," Uncle Foster said. "Most of our people are good people. They'll see what we tell them makes sense. It's the union officials who'll be the prob-lem. They can't come in and quietly work it out with us. They've got to show the membership that they're standing up to us, that they're making a fight of it. They're afraid that if they don't make a fuss, somebody will accuse them of rolling over and playing dead, and use it against them in the next union election. So they'll fight."

"But what kind of an argument can they put up, Dad?" Ernest asked.

"Oh, the usual things. They'll say we're lying, we're not losing money, we're just using foreign competition as an excuse to cut wages in order to increase our prof-its. They'll say we're really out to destroy the union. Union-busting, they'll call it. And a lot of people will believe them."

I was still thinking about what it would be like at school if there was a strike. Would they think I was on the side of the Winchester Mills just because of my name? Would they stop talking to me?

"Dad, why not show them in black and white that we're losing money?"

Uncle Foster slapped his hand softly on the desk. "Ernest. You never show your books to anyone. Ever. That's the first rule."

"Oh," Ernest said.

Uncle Foster raised his finger. "Remember, this is a

21

family business. We own it, lock, stock, and barrel. We don't have to show our books to anybody but the U.S. tax collector, and we don't show him any more than we have to, either."

"Oh," Ernest said again. "But we're losing money, aren't we?"

Uncle Foster softly smacked the desktop again and leaned forward to give us a long look. "That," he said, "is none of the union's business."

Out the window Durham had finished vacuuming the car. He got in and drove it around toward the front of the house, out of sight. There were a lot of questions going around in my head, and I couldn't answer any of them. Was the company really losing money? What was going to happen to me if there was a strike? What would my dad have done about it?

Now Uncle Foster leaned back in his chair. "Okay, I don't want you two guys to worry about any of this too much. I just wanted to warn you. Now, about this business of going after those kids in the pond. I admire your guts and all of that, but you're not to do anything of that kind again." He looked at Ernest, then me, and back at Ernest again. "You've got to get control of your temper, Ernest. You've got to learn that getting into fist fights with people isn't the way to handle these problems."

"But Dad, they didn't have the right to go into the pond." Ernest would never take anything without an argument.

"That isn't the point," Uncle Foster said. "There are better ways to handle things like that. That's what we

22

have Durham for. I didn't hire him just because he knows how to fix an engine and change a tire. I hired him because he did two tours of duty in Viet Nam. I pay him well, and it's his job to deal with problems like that."

"But Dad, we didn't want to be chicken."

Uncle Foster didn't say anything for a minute, but looked at us. Then he said, "That's the thinking of an eight-year-old, Ernest. You can't think that way at your age. This family has a lot of power, and when you have power, you use it. We don't go out brawling like drunken truck drivers. We have the courts, the law, the police—the national guard if we need it. We make sure that things around here go the way we want them to go. But we don't do it by brawling. If you do us wrong, we stay calm, we speak politely to everybody. But we move quietly. Sooner or later we'll catch you between a rock and a hard place and then you're going to feel it almighty bad."

"But those guys would have thought we were chicken if we didn't go after them."

Uncle Foster smacked his hand softly on the desktop again and leaned way forward to stare at Ernest. "Ernest." We were dead still. "In your position you do not care what people like Benny Briggs think about you. It does not matter. You are going to be very rich and very powerful. These people will never like you. They will envy you, they will defer to you, and some of them will even admire you. But they will never like you. For that you must go to your own social class. What the others think does not matter."

Until now he had been talking to both of us. But now he was talking to Ernest. As far as he was concerned I wasn't even in the room. And I wondered: Was I supposed to be one of those people whose opinion didn't matter, either?

CHAPTER 3

When my dad joined the Peace Corps they sent him down to Guatemala, because he had learned Spanish at Harvard. My mom was down there, too, and they fell in love. My mom's family were a whole lot different from the Winchesters. She was Welsh. Her grandparents came over from Wales in the 1920s, and they landed in Pittsburgh and worked in the steel mills all their lives. They never had much money. Her dad drank and spent a lot of his money in bars, and finally he got killed in a car crash when Mom was around fourteen. All her mother had after that was a small pension from the union. Her relatives never had much money, either. But Mom was smart, and she worked her way through college at night while she was a secretary during the day. Then she joined the Peace Corps.

"It was the best way I knew of getting out of that place. I couldn't stand anymore seeing those tired guys coming home from work every night with nothing to do but go down to the bar and watch the Steelers or the Pirates on TV. I couldn't take seeing my mom trying to hold the family together with nothing but that pension and whatever she could pick up cleaning for people. I saw my older sister getting married to a guy from the steel mills, six months pregnant on her wedding day, and I knew I had to get out of there. So I joined the Peace Corps and they sent me to Guatemala and I met your dad."

It was very romantic, Mom said. They got married in a little wooden chapel in a village in the mountains. I was born out there, and lived there in that little Indian village in the mountains for the first six years of my life. It's kind of hazy in my mind now, but I still have snapshots in my head of the jungle and the mountains, and the Indians we lived with—the kids running around naked, the wrinkled old grandmothers in the dirt square of the village pounding corn meal in stone troughs, the men bringing in wild boars slung upside down from poles and roasting them over a fire in the square for everybody to share. I can remember the flames leaping and sizzling as the fat dripped out of the boar; I can remember the smell of the meat cooking; I can remember the Indians getting drunk on the funny kind of beer they had and singing around the fire as the meat cooked.

But my memories are kind of tantalizing, because I can't really get the *feeling* of what it was like. I can see the snapshots, but I can't remember what it felt like to be me, a little kid growing up out there in that Indian village. One of the things I want to do most when I'm a grown-up is to go back there and see if I can get the feeling of what it was like, then.

Anyway, when I was six Mom got pregnant again.

26

She would have had the baby out there in the village with no doctor, just an Indian midwife, the way the Indians did, but there was an epidemic at the time. Dad didn't want to take a chance on it, so Mom and I flew down to Panama, where we had friends and there was a U.S. Army hospital. And the next thing we knew, a telegram came saying that Dad had died from the epidemic and they were sending his body back to the United States.

He was a hero, my dad was. He gave up being rich in order to help poor people, and he died because he wanted to stay up in the mountains and nurse the sick. He didn't have to stay there during that epidemic, but he did. The last letter Mom got from him said that he was being careful and he thought he would be all right; but what was the point of being up there with those people if he was going to turn tail and run every time there was trouble? By the time the letter came he was already dying, but we didn't know that yet.

So Mom had the baby, which turned out to be the twins. We came to the Winchester estate in Everidge and moved into the gatehouse. Uncle Foster gave Mom the job of taking care of the accounts for the house, checking the bills, paying the servants, and all that. She worked up at the big house every morning, and Uncle Foster paid her enough for us to live on, plus the gatehouse.

I worked for Durham for my spending money—during summer vacation, and during the winter all day Saturday, and sometimes after school if they had a big party coming up or some other special work. I mowed the lawns, raked leaves, weeded the gardens, helped put the storm windows up and take them down—stuff like that. It wasn't too bad. Durham always wanted things done just right, so you couldn't slip by with him; but if I did a good job, sometimes he'd let me off early.

Naturally I got to be friends with my cousin Ernest. We were the same age and even looked a little alike, except he was blond and I was dark, like Mom. Ernest always went to private schools, but when he was little they were day schools, so he was around home as much as I was, and we played together almost every afternoon—Ernest and his sister, Anne, who was a couple years younger than us. After Ernest went off to boarding school, I didn't see so much of him, but he was around for vacations and in the summer, except for August, when their whole family—Ernest and Anne and Aunt Ellen and Uncle Ernest—went off to a summer house they had in Bar Harbor, Maine. So we went on being friends.

But it wasn't like having a real friend. We always played up at his house. The gatehouse was small, and Ernest had a big room where we could make block forts or set up his trains. Ernest had every kind of toy that was ever invented. He had a huge train set with all kinds of signals and cars that unloaded themselves; he had an electric car you could ride in, which we would race up and down the upstairs hall; he had a pony to ride; he had a science kit with a Bausch and Lomb stereozoom microscope. It was great having anything you wanted to play with. The trouble was that it was all his.

None of it was mine at all. Of course Ernest and I

were always friends, and he shared his things with me. He didn't try to boss me around, and if we got into an argument about whether to play with his electric car or set up his trains, we'd choose for it. Sometimes he'd even agree to go down to my house to play; Ernest was willing to do that, because he wanted to be fair with me. But there wasn't much point in playing in our crowded little house when he had that big room and all that good stuff in it.

So in a way we were part of the family, and in a way we weren't. We always went up to the big house for Ernest's and Anne's birthdays, Thanksgiving, and Christmas, and sat there in the big dining room with a lot of people, being stared at by old Amos Winchester. But we didn't live there, and there were a lot of things that Ernest and Anne did that I wasn't in on—trips to New York, parties they went to, things like that. We lived separate, in the gatehouse.

The gatehouse was down at the end of the driveway, where it came off the road from Everidge. There was a tall, iron grillwork fence along that side of the estate, and a big gate, which nobody closed anymore. Back in the old days they'd always had a gatekeeper to stop people from coming in who didn't belong, to take messages, and to do errands. The gatehouse hadn't been meant for a whole family—just for a single man, or a couple. It was made of stone, like the big house. The twins had the original bedroom. I had a little back room, which had been meant for storage. There was a kitchen and a little living room, where Mom slept on a convertible sofa.

Actually, the gatehouse was kind of nice, except for being too small. Nobody had lived in it for years before we came, and it still had old-fashioned furniture—a big soapstone sink in the kitchen and an old round oak table we ate off with a beaded lampshade hanging down over it. Through various windows we could see the sugar maples arching over the drive, or the pine trees at the end of the pond, or the fields out back with new-cut grass. That part was pretty nice.

When you got down to it, we lived like anybody else around town—the people who worked in the mills, the people who kept stores and owned gas stations. I had a lot of friends in town, and it made me kind of uneasy when I thought about what Uncle Foster had said about "those people" not being of Ernest's social class. I felt like talking to somebody, and I decided to ride into town on my bike and see Teddy Melas. His dad had come over from Greece after World War II, when he was a kid. His mom was Greek, too. Mr. Melas worked for the Winchester Mills, in a tool room, checking out tools. They didn't have any more money than we did, and their house wasn't much bigger than ours. It was half a two-family house up on Mechanic Street, not far from the Scalzos. Teddy didn't have more things than I did; it was a lot more even between us than it was between Ernest and me.

I got to be friendly with Teddy because he was a big baseball nut like me. His dad had seen GIs playing baseball back home in Greece after the war. When he came to Massachusetts he'd got to be a big Red Sox fan. He even remembered seeing Ted Williams. Sometimes he would take Teddy up to Fenway Park for the ball games, and after Teddy and I got to be friends, he'd take me, too. I loved that, watching the game and shouting for a hit and eating hot dogs while Mr. Melas drank foamy cups of beer.

It was a nice ride. First there was the estate, with the fence along it, and cedars behind the fence, so people couldn't see in. Then you went past a couple of dairy farms, with cows grazing and corn growing and white houses and red barns. The Winchesters owned the farms and rented them out to the farmers. They lost money on the farms, but the idea was to keep developers from getting in there and putting up a shopping center or something next to the Winchester estate. After the farms you ran into a couple of gas stations and a supermarket, and then the town began. Main Street was lined with three- and four-storey old brick buildings, with offices upstairs and stores at the bottom—The Bootery, Kantor's Hardware, the Five and Ten, and such. On the side streets were the houses, mostly old, where the people who worked in the Winchester Mills lived. If you went on out the other side of town, you came to the mills—a collection of half a dozen huge factory buildings that went on for half a mile, getting newer and newer as you got farther away from town. The whole thing was surrounded by a hurricane fence. That was where all those millions and millions of dollars came from.

The wooden two-family house that the Melases lived in had a porch that ran across the front, with two doors side by side for each family's part. I'd spent so much

31

time at the Melases over the past eight years that I knew the house nearly as well as I knew my own. I knew where the loose board was on the porch; I knew about kicking the bottom of the back door to open it; I knew that you had to jiggle the handle on the toilet after you flushed it so the water wouldn't go on running.

Teddy was sitting on his front porch, putting new laces in his baseball glove. Teddy was tall and lanky and dark, and wanted to be a pitcher. I used to catch him a lot so he could work on his fork ball. "What do you say, Chris?" he said when he saw me.

I leaned my bike against the porch. "Not much," I said. I was feeling sort of nervous about raising the subject of Benny Briggs. Teddy and I didn't talk about serious stuff much. Mostly we talked about baseball. "What's the matter with your laces?"

"They were getting worn. I didn't want them breaking on me in the middle of a game." Some of the fathers who worked with Mr. Melas in his department at the mills had organized a Babe Ruth League for the kids, but I couldn't play in it, because they practiced two or three afternoons a week and I had to work for Durham. "I wish I could play," I said.

"Wouldn't Durham let you off sometimes? We don't start practice until four, when the mill lets out."

"By the time I got changed and rode into town it would be too late," I said. I climbed up onto the porch and sat down beside him. "Listen, Teddy. Did you hear anything about what happened to Benny Briggs?"

He gave me a kind of sideways look. "Yeah," he said.

32

"What did they say?"

He looked at me again. "It's going around that you and your cousin, whatever his name, sicced an attack dog on Benny. It's going around that the dog went for his throat and would have killed him, but luckily he grabbed up a stick and knocked the dog out. They said that this black guy you have up there said he would shoot Benny if he came around again."

That made me mad. "It isn't true. That's a complete lie. It didn't happen that way at all."

"Don't get mad at me, Chris. I didn't say it was true." He looked at me. "What really happened?"

I realized I'd better get the straight story going around if I could. Otherwise everybody would be sore at me when I started school in September. "It wasn't like that at all. Benny and these two other guys were swimming in the pond. My cousin went over and told them to get out. They told him to go to hell or something, and he was going to go after them. Then Durham came along with Duchess. She was on a leash the whole time. She didn't attack anybody."

"Well, I figured Benny was exaggerating."

"Durham never let go of the dog. He just told Benny and those kids to get out of there, and they took off."

"I told them there was probably another side to it. I told them that I knew you, and you wouldn't sic a dog on anybody."

It was a relief that Teddy had stuck up for me, but it worried me an awful lot that Benny was spreading his story around. "Listen, Teddy. Maybe you could start

33

telling people that Benny's lying. Maybe you could tell them you know it for a fact."

He gave me a kind of sideways look. "How could I tell them that?"

"Why not?" I said.

"Well, I don't know it for a fact. I didn't see it myself."

"Sure, I know that, Teddy," I said. Suddenly I began to wonder what he really thought about the whole thing. "But you know I wouldn't lie to you. You know if I told you what really happened it would have to be true."

"Yeah, sure. But that isn't the same as knowing it for a fact." He looked out the window and didn't say anything. Then he said, "Chris, Benny's out to get you. He's been telling everybody he's going to beat the hell out of you."

That worried me. It wasn't that I minded having to fight Benny Briggs. He was older and taller, but I weighed about as much as he did. Anyway, so what if he beat me? It would just be a fight. What I hated about it was the idea that people in town would be against me. "Well, if he wants to fight me, I'll fight him."

Teddy gave me another look. "They say he's trying to get Marie Scalzo away from you. They say he started hanging around Scalzo's store."

"Marie wouldn't go for Benny." But it made me uneasy, all the same. "Why is everybody blaming the whole thing on me? I told Ernest to let them swim there."

"Well, it looked like you were going to fight them."

34

I couldn't deny that; it was true. "They didn't have any right to swim there," I said.

Teddy didn't say anything. Then he said, "Well, you better watch out, Chris. Benny might come after you with those two other guys."

Something came to me. "Listen, Teddy. If those three guys came after me at school, would you help me fight them?"

He looked down at his baseball glove and began to work on the lacing again. "If it got started at school, somebody would stop it. Mr. Fusco or somebody would stop it."

I kept looking at him. "Yeah, but suppose they didn't. Supposed it happened after school."

"Maybe Benny will forget about it by the time school starts."

I didn't say anything for a minute. Then I said, "You mean you wouldn't fight them, Teddy?"

He looked at me. "I didn't say that. Maybe I would."

Suddenly I realized that Mr. Melas was standing in the porch doorway, listening. He was a short, dumpy guy, with a little mustache. He saw me look at him. He came out onto the porch and put his arm around me. "Chris, it isn't fair to put Teddy on the spot like that."

I didn't understand. "What spot?" I said. "If it was the other way around, I'd help him fight Benny."

He took his arm off my shoulder, but he kept hold of my arm and looked me straight in the face. "Try to understand, Chris. It's different for you. You get into some kind of trouble in town, you can always go back out to your estate, and your family will take care of you. If Teddy gets into trouble, he's got no place to go. These are our people—we don't have anybody else. We can't get into trouble with them."

I was feeling pretty confused. "But I'm from town, too. I've gone to school with Teddy and the rest of those kids for eight years. How come all of a sudden it isn't my town anymore?"

Mr. Melas put his arm around my shoulder again. "Chris, it never was your town—not in the same way that it's ours. Maybe you thought it was, but it wasn't. To all of us, you were always a little different. We always knew in the back of our minds that you were a Winchester. We always knew that you weren't really one of us."

I stood there with my mouth half-open, feeling shocked, not knowing what to say. "But what did I do wrong?"

"From where you see it, nothing," Mr. Melas said. He took his arm off my shoulder and sat down on the porch, his legs dangling down. "But in town people are saying, 'What was so bad about those kids swimming in that pond? What harm were they doing?'"

That was hard to answer. What was so bad about it? "Well, they'd leave stuff around—soda cans and food and stuff."

Mr. Melas shrugged. "People will say, 'So what, the Winchesters can afford to have somebody clean the place up.' Mind you, Chris, I'm not saying that the people in town are right, I'm not saying they're wrong. But you better understand how they feel."

I was beginning to feel kind of confused. I hadn't

36

wanted to help Ernest kick those guys out of there, but all along I'd figured he had a right to do it. It was the Winchesters' pond. But the way Mr. Melas was putting it, I wasn't so sure anymore. "Even so, it's their pond."

Mr. Melas shrugged again. "Everything in Everidge is theirs," he said. "They own the mills and the bank and half the houses the people live in. You don't get elected to anything around here unless they say so. You think the cops would do anything the Winchesters didn't like?" He stopped and looked at me some more, and then he said, "Chris, you got to understand, people around here don't like your family. They remember what happened in thirty-seven, during the Depression."

"Mr. Melas, that isn't fair. That was fifty years ago or something."

"The old people remember. They remember living on boiled potatoes. They remember being in breadlines to get handouts. Some people's pride is still bad hurt by that. The Winchesters don't know what it's like to take handouts to feed your family. Maybe if they'd done something since to make up for it, people would forget, but what have they done? And now they're going to try to bust the union and cut wages."

"Mr. Melas, why am I getting the blame? It doesn't have anything to do with me."

"Your name's Winchester, Chris. That'll be enough for most people around here."

CHAPTER 4

I stuck around the Melases for a little while and then I said I had to get home for supper. I was feeling pretty bad. That's one of the worst things there is, to find out that a lot of people hate you—to find out that everywhere you went there would be enemies. I just wished Ernest hadn't started anything with those guys. I wished I'd told him I wasn't going to help him, and not even gone over to the pond with him. Although from what Mr. Melas said, that probably wouldn't have done any good. My name was Winchester. I wondered if I ought to change my name. Would that do any good? Mom wouldn't like that very much, though.

What about Marie Scalzo? Would she start hating me? Marie and I had a lot of fun together. She was short and cute and had long, black hair that came halfway down to her waist. She was interested in nature. She was always taking books out of the library on wildflowers and trees and birds, and on Saturday mornings she went on these nature walks they had, where they would go on one of the school buses to a lake or a forest preserve somewhere to study it. At least she went when it wasn't too busy at the store and her dad would let her get away.

On Sundays she and I would go on nature walks of our own. We'd ride our bikes out to someplace where she'd been, and we'd walk around holding hands while she explained everything to me. Then we'd sit down in the middle of the woods all by ourselves and eat lunch. That was one advantage of having a girlfriend whose family owned a grocery store. She always brought terrific lunches—deviled eggs and turkey sandwiches and fresh doughnuts.

There was one special place we went to a lot, a little state forest about five miles outside of town, where there was a meadow in the middle of the woods that was always full of wildflowers. We'd sit at the edge of the woods to eat our lunch, with the sun coming through the leaves onto us like pennies, looking out at the flowers all red and blue and white. It was beautiful. Then after we'd eaten we'd lie down together and kiss. I'd start to feel sexy and I'd hint something about it. But it wasn't any use hinting anything like that to Marie. She was Catholic, and didn't even like me to say "damn" or "hell." As far as sex was concerned, she always said she wasn't ready for it yet, she wanted to wait. I didn't even bother to argue with her about it because I knew she would never change her mind, and arguing would only get us into a fight. But she liked me, and she liked to kiss, all right.

And now what? Was she going to become my enemy? Would she start going around with Benny Briggs? What about the rest of the family—her father, her mother, her younger sister, her older brother, Frankie. I figured Frankie was bound to be on Benny's side. Frankie was only a couple of years ahead of me in school, but he'd got left back once and was older than that. Mr. Scalzo wanted him to go into the store with him and take it over when it was time for Mr. Scalzo to retire. Frankie was a kind of good-natured guy that everybody liked, but not nearly as smart as Marie. He was more Briggs's type and would take his side, I figured.

But I didn't think Marie would. Benny wasn't her type. I figured he wouldn't go around with any girl who wouldn't let him have sex with her. That was the kind of guy he was. But still, even if she didn't start going with Benny, would she take his side against me because my name was Winchester?

When I got back to the gatehouse Mom was in the kitchen, frying chicken. It smelled pretty good. I sat down at the old oak table. It was always sort of dark in the gatehouse because the windows were small, and the beaded lamp that hung down over the table was on a lot of the time. Out the window I could see the sun, kind of red, going down over the pine trees by the pond. The window was open, and when the breeze blew a little, I could smell fresh-cut hay along with the frying chicken.

"What else are we having?" I asked.

"Spinach," she said. "And corn bread." She had a way of making corn bread she had learned from the Indians in Guatemala that I really liked. She said we'd eaten it almost every day when we were down there. I liked the way Mom looked. She was thirty-eight, but she still looked pretty young. She had a dark face like mine and dark brown hair, which she wore in braids the way Indians did.

I had a habit of talking things over with Mom when I was confused about something. Mom always had clear ideas about what people should do and what they shouldn't. She'd had a hard upbringing and was pretty realistic about things. And she didn't talk down to me—she always talked to me like I was grown up. I figured that was because, since Dad died, she didn't have another grown-up around to talk to, and had to use me for that. I decided to get into all of this stuff about Benny Briggs.

She twisted away from the stove and looked at me over her shoulder. "What did Uncle Foster have to say?"

"It was sort of complicated," I said. "He wasn't sore at us for going after those guys, but he said he didn't want us to do it anymore. He said we were supposed to be better than that, or something."

"What did he mean by that exactly?"

"He said he was paying Durham to handle that stuff and we should stay out of it. He said we shouldn't solve problems by brawling like drunken truck drivers."

She went on turning over chicken in the frying pan. "I agree with him there for once. You and Ernest should have better sense than to take on some tough kids from town."

There was something wrong about that. Wasn't I a kid from town? I decided I'd better not tell her that

Benny was out looking for me. She'd get all upset. "They weren't so tough. I know one of them."

"All the more reason for staying out of trouble," she said. "What else did Uncle Foster say?"

"He said there might be a strike. Did you know about that?"

She bent over to look under the frying pan and lowered the flame. Then she came over and sat down at the table with me. "There's been a lot of talk about it. That's all anybody knows."

"From the way Uncle Foster was talking, it sounded like there was a good chance of it. He said there might be violence."

"Let's hope not," Mom said. She looked at the big old clock on the wall and frowned. "The twins ought to be home by now."

"Where are they?"

"Casey took them swimming." Casey was one of the maids. She liked kids because she didn't have any of her own, and because she figured we were basically servants like her, she didn't mind doing things for us.

"Listen, Mom, tell me about that time during the Depression, when they closed the mills. Did they really have to do it?"

"What got you thinking about that?"

"Something Mr. Melas said. He said that the old people around town haven't forgotten about it. He said a lot of people in town don't like the Winchesters." I decided not to say anything about not liking me, either. "Did Dad ever say anything about that?"

"He didn't talk about his family very much. He was

42

wrapped up in his work, and that's what he talked about. Down there in Guatemala the Winchester Mills seemed pretty faraway."

It came to me that one of Dad's reasons for going into the Peace Corps in the first place was because he didn't like a lot of the things the Winchesters had done. That was the kind of guy he was. I wished he were there to tell me about it. I sat there, feeling sad that I couldn't remember more about him than I did. He was always busy, always going off here and there to little Indian villages to show them how to purify their water or fertilize their crops, or which medicines to take. Most of what I remember about him wasn't memories at all, but stuff from the pictures that Mom had in a photo album of those years we were in Guatemala. I just wished he could come back again, even if it were only for a day, so I could ask him questions and see what he was really like.

I shook him out of my mind. "I wish I knew the truth of it. Mr. Melas says that during the Depression people lived on boiled potatoes and handouts from the breadline."

"I wouldn't worry about it if I were you, Chris. It was a long time ago."

"Mom, did Dad believe that the Winchesters were doing something wrong? Did he believe that they were too hard on the people who worked for them? Is that why he joined the Peace Corps?"

She gave me a quick look. "Where have you been getting these ideas from?"

"No place," I said. "I just have a feeling about it."

She looked me in the face. "Chris, so long as we're accepting your uncle Foster's hospitality, I don't think we ought to talk about them that way."

"What hospitality are we accepting?"

"This house," she said, waving around her cooking fork. "Our car. Lots of things."

"But you work for it, Mom. You work up at the big house every day."

"Part-time. I work part-time. I don't earn enough to support this place, three kids, a house, clothes, food. One person can't support a family like that on a part-time job. Who do you think paid for our car? Who do you think pays for gas, and for the taxes on this place? Your uncle Foster has been very generous with us. I don't think we ought to start bad-mouthing him."

I could see that, but still, there was something that bothered me about it. "Maybe we shouldn't take so much from them. Maybe we shouldn't live here." I was thinking: If we moved into town and weren't part of the Winchesters anymore, the kids might see me as being more like them.

"Maybe we should," she said. She got up, fished around in the cabinet over the sink, and took out a bottle of sherry she kept there. Mom never drank very much, but sometimes when she got upset she drank a glass of sherry. She poured some sherry into an orange juice glass and sat down at the oak table again. "We could move into town and I could take a full-time job. But then I wouldn't have much time left for you or the twins. You don't need me so much now, but they do. Remember, I'm the only parent they have. And of course you'd have to get a real job—working in the mills, probably, instead of keeping the grounds with Durham. It wouldn't be so nice."

What would Dad have done? I wondered. How I wished I could ask him. "Mom, there must have been something about the Winchester business that Dad didn't like, or he wouldn't have gone off and joined the Peace Corps."

She didn't say anything for a minute, but sat there looking down into her sherry glass, thinking. "Chris, your dad knew that to be in business you had to be ruthless sometimes. He knew that the company could be very tough when they had to, and sometimes a lot of innocent bystanders got hurt."

"What do you mean by that?"

"Well, you take this situation with the foreign competition. It isn't the Winchesters' fault that the Koreans or Taiwanese or somebody else can pay their workers a lot less than the Winchesters can here in America. But that's the situation they're faced with, and they're going to do what they have to do to survive. And if it means cutting wages, or even closing down the electronics division, they'll do it, no matter how many people lose their jobs. Your father knew that the Winchesters run the business out of self-interest. They're not a charitable institution. No business is. He wasn't against it, necessarily. He just didn't want to be involved himself. He always said he didn't want to spend his life trying to figure out a way to make an extra dollar."

I thought about it for a minute. Then I said, "Mom, are they *really* losing money because of foreign compe-

45

tition? Do they *really* have to cut wages?"

She didn't say anything, but took a sip of her sherry and thought about it. "Chris, nobody will ever know, except Skipper and your uncle Foster and a few others at the top."

The whole thing didn't sit right. If the people at the top who ran things didn't have to worry about doing right by other people, who did? "Mom, if it wasn't right for Dad, why is it right for anybody?"

She was getting cross with me, I could see that. "Chris, people are different. People don't all look at things the same way. You're not the same person as your dad."

"Well, but maybe I think like him," I said. "I mean, if something's wrong for me, it should be wrong for everybody."

She stared at me. "Why? What right do you have to decide what everybody's morality should be?" She finished off her sherry. "Well, this isn't getting supper cooked." She went to the stove and began turning the chicken again.

But it still didn't sit right. "Mom, look. The Winchesters—"

She whirled around from the stove, her hands on her hips, the big fork she had been turning the chicken with dripping grease on the floor. "Chris, I don't want to hear any more of this. I want an end to it right now."

I was pretty surprised. Mom didn't blow up like that very much. Mostly she kept cool. If there was a problem between us, she'd sit down with me and she'd give her side of it, and I'd give mine. But this time she was

46

plain angry, and I couldn't see the reason for it. What had I done? "Mom, I can say what I want."

She bit her lip, and then she said in a quiet voice, "Chris, don't you realize that Uncle Foster might make a place for you in the business if you show promise? Don't you understand that if you do well in school he might send you to Harvard? Don't you know that if you did well at Harvard he might bring you into the business—not just as an ordinary employee, but as somebody who can go to the top? Don't you realize any of that?"

I sat there, feeling shocked. It was kind of a numb feeling, like everything in the world had come to a stop. Nothing that Mom had just said had ever occurred to me at all. I'd never thought much about what I would do when I grew up, except maybe try to make it as a professional baseball player, which wasn't actually too realistic. Or maybe go into social service, the way Dad did. But it had never occurred to me that I could go into the business with Ernest. "Mom, Ernest's going to inherit the business and the house and everything. Ernest and Anne."

"He might. And he might not. A lot of things could happen. Look what happened to Uncle Foster. He grew up thinking that your dad would get it, and then your dad announced he was going into the Peace Corps and it landed in Uncle Foster's lap. Or look at your great-great-uncle Asa, the one who ran away to Paris to become a Bohemian. He lost out, too. It's happened twice in this century. It could happen again."

But I knew Ernest. He wasn't the type to go into the

Peace Corps. He liked to fight too much. He was already training himself to be boss of the mills. "Ernest wouldn't do that."

She thought about it. "No, he wouldn't, that's true. It would be out of character. But things happen. A car accident . . . "

"Mom."

"All right, I didn't mean that. I'm certainly not wishing anything like that on Ernest. The odds are that he'll take over when he grows up. All I'm saying is that life is unpredictable."

I was feeling very strange. The whole world had changed. I wasn't sure I liked it. It was like the taste of electricity, kind of interesting, but sour. "Do you really mean that if Ernest—if Ernest decided to be a painter or something—I'd get it? I'd get the whole thing—the mills, the big house, all that money, everything?"

"It isn't that simple, Chris. In a powerful family like the Winchesters, they don't think of the wealth as belonging to anybody in particular. It belongs to the family as a whole. The way they see it, whoever is head of the family has the responsibility to preserve the wealth and the power, and increase it if possible. But the head of the family makes the final decisions. That's why they're always so careful to make sure that they don't put somebody incompetent in the job. If the first son isn't up to it, they'll pass right over him. They'll give it to the second son or a nephew or a son-in-law or a cousin."

"Uncle Foster will give it to Ernest," I said. "He won't give it to me."

She shrugged. "It won't be entirely up to Uncle Foster. Skipper turned the day-to-day operations of the mills over to Uncle Foster a few years ago, but Skipper's still got the final say. You've got to remember, you're just as much his grandchild as Ernest is."

I'd never thought about it that way. It had always seemed to me that Skipper was more Ernest's grandfather than he was mine. He'd lived in the big house when Ernest was a little kid and I'd been growing up in Guatemala. Ernest knew him much better than I did. But it was true—he was as much my grandfather as Ernest's. "What about Anne?"

"The Winchesters are not about to turn the company over to a woman, you can count on that." She thought for a minute. "Look, Chris, even if Ernest goes on to take over, that doesn't mean you'll be cut out. Ernest will need help, he'll need people around him he can trust, and that means members of the family. Besides, they'll want somebody available in case something does happen to him. Suppose Ernest were to die early, before the next generation was ready to step in. They'd want to have somebody like you on tap to fill in. The whole point is that if you show promise, if you work hard at school and do the things they expect of you, they'll take care of you."

"I'd be rich?"

"If you were rising up in the company they'd make sure you had plenty of money, because they would want you to have a life-style suitable for a Winchester—a big house, expensive cars, the best clothes, riding horses if you wanted or a ski lodge or whatever. They

49

wouldn't want you living in a gatehouse and driving an eight-year-old car."

I sat there saying nothing for a minute. Then I said, "It all seems so strange and new to me, Mom. I just never thought of it."

"Chris, I'm surprised you never thought about it before. I thought you were aware of these things."

"No. It seems so strange. I figured that Dad had given it all up and we were just lucky that Uncle Foster let us live in the gatehouse."

She leaned over and ran her hand through my hair.

"Poor Chris. Life is full of shocks. I guess we should have talked about it before."

Then we heard Casey coming along with the twins and we stopped talking about it. But that night, when I lay in bed in my little room, looking out at the moon rising through the leaves of the maple tree and lighting up the field beyond, I couldn't sleep. I felt strange —good and bad all at once. I felt like I had just come into the world again, a different person. I kept thinking: What if Ernest decided to be a painter and the big house were mine? What if I owned five cars and sat in Uncle Foster's office telling Durham to get the limo ready, I wanted to go to Logan Airport and fly to Paris? What if? I knew one thing, though: If anything like that were to happen, I couldn't go on. I'd have to make up my mind whose side I was on.

CHAPTER 5

Two days later I was mowing around the white cast-iron table and chairs that sat on the grass by the side of the pond. My mind was still full of what Mom had told me, and ideas kept going through my head about how strange it would be twenty years from now, if I was living in the big house, remembering the time when I was still a kid, mowing that lawn I was standing on. What would I be like then? What would it be like to be rich and powerful?

I cut up to the lawn furniture, and then I stopped the mower so I could move a cast-iron chair out of the way. At that moment, out of the corner of my eye, I got a glimpse of something over near the edge of the pine grove by the pond. I set down the chair I had picked up, straightened up, and looked.

The edge of the pine grove was maybe thirty yards away, but I could see something there that seemed out of place. It looked like a chunk of wet black log or a heap of weeds. Whatever it was, it was my job to clean it up. So I shut off the mower and trotted over to have a look.

As I got closer I began to see that it was some kind of

51

animal—a skunk, maybe, or a woodchuck. Then I realized that it was a whole lot bigger than a woodchuck. Suddenly I saw what it was and I began running. In a minute I was looking down at Duchess.

Her head was twisted back in a strange way. There was foam around her muzzle, and her eyes were wide open. But there was no light in them, and I knew that she was dead. My heart started to thump. I turned and ran up across the lawn, around the house on the bluestone driveway, and into the stable.

The stable boy was sweeping up. "Where's Durham?" I shouted.

He didn't let go of the broom, but gestured with his chin. "Out back. In the cutting garden."

I ran out of the stable and around back. Durham was in the garden, bent over the dahlias. "Durham," I shouted, "Duchess is down by the pond. I think she's dead."

He jerked upright. "Dead?"

"I think so."

"Where?"

"I'll show you." We ran back around the stable, down the driveway, and across the lawn to the pine grove. I pointed. "She's in there." Durham ran on, and when he came up to the dog he dropped to his knees and knelt there, his hand on Duchess's muzzle.

"Poisoned. Those lousy punks poisoned her."

"Who, Durham?"

"Them." He stood up and spat into the pine needles. "Them. The ones I chased out of here the other day. Sure as you're standing there, they did it."

52

"You don't think she just died, Durham?"

"There wasn't nothing wrong with her yesterday. They come in here last night and did it. Those lousy punks. To kill a dog like that. They wouldn't take on no man. Just a poor dumb dog that didn't know any better than to eat a chunk of poisoned meat." He knelt down and began to stroke the dog's fur. "Don't you worry none, old girl," he said softly. "We'll get them for you." He stayed there for a minute stroking her, almost as if he could hardly stand to say good-bye. Then he stood up. "Stay here and watch. Don't let nobody touch nothing." He trotted off swiftly up the lawn toward the house.

I stood there feeling scared and sorry. I didn't like looking at Duchess with her head twisted back and the dried foam on her muzzle, and I turned my back to her and looked out over the pond. Did Benny Briggs really poison Duchess? Was he the kind of guy who would do something like that? I wasn't sure about that. Benny was the kind of guy who would hit you if he was sore at you—he wouldn't think of something like poisoning a dog. It seemed to me more likely that it was some grown-ups. Maybe Benny's dad had done it, or some of his dad's friends. But maybe it had nothing to do with Benny. Maybe poor Duchess had just got hold of some rat poison somehow. I hoped it wasn't Benny. There was going to be all kinds of trouble if it was.

About five minutes later Ernest came charging across the lawn. The minute he saw Duchess he began cursing Benny Briggs. "Ernest," I said, "we don't know if Benny did it. It could have been an accident."

"Come on, Chris, who else would do it except Benny? We're going to get that guy, all right. Oh, he's going to be sorry he started all this."

The whole thing was beginning to bother me a lot. I was sorry for Duchess. It was terrible to see her lying there all twisted back, knowing that she must have been hurting something awful when she was dying. But even so, the Winchesters were going to take it out on Benny. They were going to make things mighty tough for him. I was beginning to get a little smarter about the Winchesters. I was beginning to understand that they could be very tough and hard when they wanted to. If they were willing to let a lot of people lose their jobs, what they did to one dumb kid who didn't understand how anything worked wouldn't bother them very much. "Ernest, give the guy a break. You can't prove that he did it."

"We'll prove it," Ernest said. "Don't worry about that."

Uncle Foster came with Durham, and in a little while the vet drove up in his van. We all stood around while the vet squatted over Duchess. "Looks like poisoning," he said finally. "But I won't know for sure until I do an autopsy." He and Durham wrapped Duchess in a piece of canvas and carried her up the lawn to the van.

Uncle Foster touched my arm. "Chris, come on back to the office with me. I want to talk to you."

I didn't want to go with him. He was going to put me in the middle of the whole thing. I hated the idea of that. I didn't like Benny Briggs very much now, but I didn't want to take sides against him, either. But there was nothing I could do, so I followed Uncle Foster up the lawn, into the house, and down to his office, with the antique desk and the pictures of those ships on the walls. I sat down in the easy chair, and Uncle Foster went behind his desk, put his feet up on his wastebasket, and looked out the window. The limo was parked there, and there was a bucket of water and a sponge beside it, but Durham had gone into town with the vet.

Uncle Foster went on looking out the window. "Chris, what do you know about these people?"

"Not too much, Uncle Foster. Benny isn't in my grade. I never knew him too well."

"What about the others?"

"I don't know them at all. I think they might even be older than Benny. I mean, I see them around, but I don't know who they are." That was almost true—I didn't know the name of one of them, and I wasn't sure about the name of the other.

"But you played ball with the Briggs kid, right?"

"That's when I knew him, when we were on the team together. I never hung out with him or anything like that."

"That's all you know?"

"I guess so," I said. "But it doesn't seem like Benny is the type of guy who would poison a dog."

He glanced around at me and then looked back out the window. "Chris, why are you protecting these people?"

That stopped me. I didn't know how to answer it. Finally I said, "I just don't want to be put in the middle."

"Chris, they come onto our place to swim without asking, and when we tell them to leave, they poison our dog. We didn't threaten them, we didn't use any force against them, did we? You were there—Durham didn't turn the dog on them, did he?"

"No. He just shouted at them to get out of there."

"They're the ones who caused the trouble. There's no middle to be in, Chris. They're wrong, and we're right."

I wondered if he understood "these people" any better than Ernest did. It didn't sound like he did, but I wasn't sure. "See, the thing is, Uncle Foster, I go to school with these guys. I'm going to be in high school next year, and Benny Briggs will be there, too. I can't help being in the middle."

He turned his head around and looked at me for a minute, thinking. "Yes, of course," he said. "I keep forgetting that. In some ways you're a town boy, aren't you, Chris? I should have recognized that before."

"Lots of those guys are my friends." I decided not to say anything about Marie. I didn't know why, but I didn't want to mention her to him.

"Yes, of course they would be." He nodded to himself a couple of times, thinking. "It's our fault you're in the middle, when you get down to it. Perhaps we should have done things another way."

I knew what he meant by that—he meant that they should have sent me to a private school, like Ernest. But there wasn't anything I could say, and anyway, the way things were going, I wasn't sure I wanted to be sent to a private school.

Uncle Foster nodded to himself again. "I guess we've

been taking you a little too much for granted, Chris. You know, six years ago Skipper turned the mills over to me, and it's kept me pretty busy. I keep forgetting that you haven't got a father. I should remind myself of that a little more. I think if Skipper had been around a little more, he'd have seen that more was done for you. Your grandfather's very pleased with the way you've been growing up, Chris. I hope you realize that. So am I, for that matter."

I hadn't realized it, and it surprised me a lot. In fact, I hadn't realized that Skipper ever gave me a thought one way or another. But now I could see that he had, and more than that, he'd talked about me with Uncle Foster. It surprised me, all right, but it made me feel good, too. I didn't know what to say. "Well, thanks, Uncle Foster."

He nodded to himself once more. Then he said, "Now having said all that, Chris, you've got to see our viewpoint, too." He took his feet off the wastebasket and turned around to face me. "These people have got to be reminded that there are laws in this country about private property. I can't walk into their houses and help myself to their refrigerators, and they can't come up here whenever they like and use my pond."

He wagged his finger at me. "We're going to find out who poisoned that dog, and then we'll decide what to do. In this town things go the way we want them to go." He didn't say this in a loud voice, or thump on the desk with his fist or anything. He said it calmly, like he was talking about the weather, but I knew he meant every word of it.

"Maybe Benny Briggs didn't do it," I said. "I don't think he's the type of guy would poison a dog."

Uncle Foster swiveled away to face out the window again. He put his feet on the wastebasket and touched the tips of his fingers together in front of his chin. "Chris, power is a very interesting thing, as you might find out one day. If you do, you'll quickly come to learn that it's like a muscle in the body—if you don't use it, it deteriorates. If you allow people to erode your power, pretty soon you won't have it anymore, and somebody else will. Then you'll be at their mercy, and that's not as much fun as the other way around. I'm sorry about Duchess, because I liked that dog, but she was more Durham's than mine." He clicked the tips of his fingers together a couple of times. "But that's not the point. The point is that I can't let anyone injure us, without striking back. And that's what I'm going to do. I'm going to find out who did this, and I'm going to punish them for it." He turned his head to look at me. "Can you understand that, Chris?"

I didn't like it, but I understood it. "Yes, I see what you mean, Uncle Foster."

Suddenly he stood up. "Okay. I hope next time we have a conversation it'll be on a pleasanter subject."

I went out of there feeling pretty confused. I could see that there was something to all that stuff about not letting people erode your power. It was pretty much the same as not running away from a fight—if you ran away once, people would always be picking on you, because they would figure you wouldn't fight back. But something about the whole thing bothered me. I

58

couldn't quite get hold of what it was. It kept coming to the edge of my brain and then slipping away before I could grab it. Normally I would have talked something like this over with Mom, but I wasn't so sure about that now. I had the feeling that she would take Uncle Foster's side. I didn't want to get into another argument with her about the Winchesters.

But I needed somebody to talk to, and I decided to go see Marie Scalzo. Suddenly I realized that I hadn't seen her since all of this had started. I wondered why. Usually if we missed seeing each other for a couple of days, one of us would call the other one. But I hadn't called her, and she hadn't called me. That was funny. Why hadn't I called her? Why hadn't she called me?

Durham was still gone with the vet. I went back down to where I'd been working when I'd spotted Duchess and finished up the mowing. Durham wasn't back yet, and he hadn't told me what he wanted me to do next. I went down to the gatehouse, ate some lunch, and then I got on my bike and rode into town, past the cedars that ran along the estate, past the dairy farms that came next. It was hot, and the breeze I got from riding felt good. Finally I came into Main Street, went by the Five and Ten, The Bootery, and turned up Mechanic Street. Scalzo's Grocery was a couple of blocks up, in a neighborhood of two- and three-storey wooden houses that the Winchesters had built for the workers during World War I. Business was booming then, because of the war, and they had had to provide housing to get workers to come to Everidge from Boston, Hartford, and New York. One family lived on each floor. I'd been in these places often enough, visiting guys from school, and I knew what they were like. They'd have two bedrooms usually, one for the kids and one for the parents. There'd be a living room, dining room, and kitchen with linoleum, a cracked sink, and old refrigerator. They were comfortable enough places, but not very big, and if there were a lot of kids in the family, somebody would have to sleep in the living room on a convertible sofa. But people liked living in those places because they were cheap. If they got laid off for some reason, they could usually scrape together enough money to make the rent.

Scalzo's Grocery was in the bottom floor of one of those buildings. The family lived upstairs over the store. They were lucky, because there were a couple of storerooms behind the store. Marie's brother, Frankie, slept in one of those rooms, so Marie and her little sister could have the bedroom upstairs.

I stopped in front of the store and locked my bike to a telephone pole. Then I went in. It was an old store. Mr. Scalzo had got it from a relative or something, and it had been around for a long time, since right after World War II. There were shelves of cans and packages around three sides of it—cans of coffee and jars of mustard and boxes of rice and flour. Across the back was the delicatessen case, and a marble counter ran down one side. The counter was loaded with baskets of pepperoni, wheels of cheese, a carton of bread, a jar of pickles. I liked going in there; it smelled spicy and delicious. Mr. Scalzo said it was rough competing against the supermarkets because he couldn't match their

60

prices, but a lot of people felt more comfortable going into a family store, especially if they could run up a bill and pay it off every two weeks on payday.

Mr. Scalzo was talking to a customer at the counter, and Marie was behind the delicatessen case, weighing out a chunk of parmesan cheese for an old woman. She didn't notice me come in, an I stood there by the door, watching her. She was wearing a white apron over her T-shirt and jeans, smudged in a couple of spots with mustard where she'd wiped her hands after making somebody a sandwich. She said something to the woman in Italian. Then she took the piece of cheese off the scales, put it down on a sheet of white butcher paper, and began to wrap it up. She'd done it so often, her hands twinkled as they flew around the cheese, and her dark brown hair wavered a little as she tipped her head this way and that to see that she had got the hunk of cheese properly wrapped. I liked watching her do it. She looked cute, concentrating like that.

She handed the cheese to the old woman and then she noticed me. "Hi," she said.

"Hi," I said. I walked back to the counter. She got out a salami, turned on the slicer, and began to slice it. "Can you get away for a little while, or are you stuck?"

She glanced at her dad. "Maybe," she said. "In a couple of minutes." I stood off to the side to be out of the way. In a minute she finished with the old woman. She rang up the amount and counted out the change. Then she took off her apron, bundling it up on the shelf under the counter. "Dad, I'm going out back with Chris for a minute," she said.

"Don't be long," he said.

We went through the back of the store, into a kind of dirt backyard they had. Grass wouldn't grow there. An old ash tree grew in the middle of it, and under the ash tree Mr. Scalzo had built a picnic table and benches. They had a charcoal grill, and hot summer nights they'd cook hot dogs and hamburgers out there. I'd eaten with them plenty of times there.

We sat down at the picnic table facing each other, holding hands. "What happened between you and Benny Briggs, Chris?"

"How did you know about that?"

"Everybody knows," she said. "It's all over town. Everybody's talking about it. Benny and his dad are making a big thing out of it."

I hated to hear that. It was going to put me in the middle even worse. "I wish everybody wouldn't make such a big deal out of it. Benny and those guys were swimming in the pond, and my cousin told them to get out."

She frowned. "That's not what Benny says. He says the caretaker sicced a dog on them. Benny said he picked up a branch and clubbed the dog, otherwise he'd have torn them to pieces."

"That's completely untrue," I said. I was beginning to feel sore. It was bad enough as it was—why did Benny have to make it worse? "It wasn't like that at all. The caretaker heard the noise and came out with the dog. He kept the dog on the leash the whole time."

"Well, that's not what Benny says."

62

I looked at her. "Are you going to believe me or Benny Briggs?"

She looked down. "Don't get sore at me. I didn't say that. Benny did."

"Well, who do you believe?" I said. "Me or Benny?"

"No, I believe you, Chris. What exactly happened?"

"Just what I said. My cousin and I were walking down to the gatehouse and we heard this noise in the pond. He wanted to go in after Benny. I tried to talk him out of it, but I couldn't. Then the caretaker came."

"Benny says you and your cousin jumped in after them with sticks."

"Not true. We never went into the water." I didn't want to lie to her if I could help it. "We would have gone after them, but we didn't have any sticks. It would have been two of us against three. But then the caretaker came." I hoped that it being two against three would give her some idea that we had been willing to take a pretty big chance. "Did you know that somebody came up there last night and poisoned the dog? I found her this morning."

"I wouldn't blame them," she said. "If it was me, I'd have done it, too."

"Marie, didn't you hear me the first time? Durham didn't sic the dog on anyone. That's a lie."

"Don't shout, Chris. Everybody can hear you."

"Well, I'm sick of the whole thing. Benny's making up this whole story so he'll be in the right. He had no business going up there to swim, anyway."

"What was the harm in it?" Marie said. She was

beginning to get mad, too. We were headed for a fight, which was exactly what I didn't want. I just wanted somebody to talk to who understood my point of view. But it didn't seem like she did, any more than Uncle Foster did. "Marie, they can't let anybody come out to swim who wants to."

"Benny and those guys weren't hurting anything. Why should the Winchesters have that whole pond to themselves?"

I didn't say anything. There was nothing but trouble coming out of the whole thing, and I didn't know how to stop it. "Marie, please, let's not fight about it. Benny Briggs is lying. He's making a whole big thing about it. My cousin just told them to get out. Benny mouthed off at him. My cousin has a quick temper and he wanted to get Benny. It was just a fight between a couple of kids."

"I heard you fought Benny, too."

"Nobody fought anybody. The caretaker came with the dog before—"

"So he did sic the dog on them."

"No, he didn't," I said. "Why don't you believe me? He just brought the dog along to throw a scare into them. They jumped out and left. That was all there was to it."

"But you would have fought Benny if the caretaker hadn't brought the dog."

When I'd come down there, I'd hoped that Marie would understand the thing better than the other people had, but she didn't. She didn't understand Cousin Ernest any more than Ernest understood her. She couldn't see that the Winchesters might be in the right. She couldn't see that the Winchesters might be in the right on anything. Now I realized why she hadn't called me. It was because I'd sided with the Winchesters against one of the town people. As far as she was concerned that was wrong. She couldn't see it any other way.

"Look, Marie, can't you understand that the Winchesters were in the right? People can't just go walking onto other people's property without permission. I mean, what if my cousin walked into your house and helped himself out of your refrigerator?" Suddenly I realized that I was talking like Uncle Foster, and I began to feel hot and prickly. I didn't want to take my ideas from him.

Marie didn't say anything. She just sat there looking at me for a long time. I looked back. Then she took her hand away from me and said, "Chris, Dad says I shouldn't go out with you. He says you're a Winchester and someday you'll go off with your own kind. He says that sooner or later you'll let me down. He says that even if you didn't want to, the Winchesters would put pressure on you to go around with your own kind. He says that they'd never let you marry a girl whose dad owns a grocery store."

The whole thing was making me feel very upset —part angry because she was saying things about me that weren't true, part worried that I'd lose her, and part scared that all the people I'd known for years were turning against me for something that I didn't do.

"Marie, what do you mean, my own kind of people? I'm not anybody's kind of people. I'm just me." I was beginning to shout.

"You're a Winchester, Chris," she shouted back.

"I don't go to private school. I go to the same school as you and Benny Briggs and the rest of you go to. Why am I supposed to be some different kind of people from you?"

"What about when you grow up? Are you going to get a job in the mills? Are you going to go to work in a grocery store slicing salami and dishing out potato salad?"

There she was right, and I knew it. I wouldn't necessarily go into the family business and become an executive—I didn't know if I would want to, and anyway, the way this whole business was going, Uncle Foster might not trust me anymore. But I wouldn't go work in the mills on the line or spend my days dishing out potato salad. If I didn't go into the business, I'd probably get into some kind of social service, the way my dad did. Something like that. But I wouldn't be dishing out potato salad. And Marie would.

I said, "Maybe I'll join the Peace Corps, the way my dad did. You don't know what I might do."

"But you won't have to go to work in the mills."

I looked down at my hands. "No, that's true. My uncle would never let me do that."

"Then you'll let me down, because like goes to like, Dad says."

I looked at her. "My dad didn't go to like. He married my mom, and her folks worked in the steel mills in Pittsburgh."

Suddenly she crumpled in on herself. She hunched forward, her shoulders got smaller, and she put her hands over her face. "Oh, Chris," she said, "it isn't me. It's Dad. He's afraid you'll talk me into having sex with you, and then you'll go off with your own and let me down. That's what worries him. He doesn't want me to start having sex with somebody who's likely to let me down."

It didn't seem to me that Mr. Scalzo would have talked about stuff like that to Marie. "Did he say that to you?"

"No. Mom told me. She said they were both worried about that."

"Marie, I never tried to talk you into having sex."

She still had her hands over her face. She nodded. "I know. But I knew you wanted to, and maybe someday I would have changed my mind."

Suddenly I got the idea that there was something more to it than she was saying. It wasn't her folks that she was thinking about. What she really wanted was for me to promise that I'd never let her down. She wanted to know if she could trust me. She was saying all that stuff about like going to like to get me to promise I wouldn't walk out on her someday. And from the way she was talking, I had the feeling that if I did make some kind of promise, she might have sex with me.

But I couldn't promise her that I'd never let her down, because I didn't know if I would. I couldn't promise her anything like that. I sat there feeling lousy about myself. The only thing I could think of to say was, "Marie, I don't want to break up with you. I just want to keep on going the way we were going. Let's not let this whole Benny Briggs thing break us up. That was between Benny and my cousin. It didn't have anything to do with me."

Suddenly she jumped up, came around the picnic table, and put her arms around my neck. "Oh, Chris, I'm so confused," she said. Then she started to cry. She hugged me tight. "I love you, Chris."

I'd never seen her cry before. I got up and we stood there hugging. I could feel my heart beating like crazy where she was pressed up against me. "I love you," I said.

We stood there for a minute and then she broke away. She wiped her tears with her hand. "I have to get back to the store." I took her hand, and we walked around the side of the house to the street. Benny Briggs was standing on the sidewalk out front, looking in through the window in the door to see if Marie was there.

CHAPTER 6

We stopped dead. For just a moment Benny didn't notice us, but went on looking in the store. Then he realized we were standing there, and he turned around. He didn't say anything, but just looked at us. I looked back, trying to figure out how to fight him. He was a lot taller than me—tall and gangly, with a long reach—but I didn't think he was much heavier than I was. With that reach there wouldn't be much use in trying to box him. I didn't know much about boxing, anyway. The best thing would be to tackle him and then see if I could get on top of him.

Benny said, "What are you doing with that guy, Marie? He's not your kind. You should stay with your own people."

That surprised me. It didn't sound like something Benny would think up on his own. It sounded like something he'd heard somewhere. I said, "It's none of your business who she goes around with, Briggs."

"Winchester, we don't want you people in this part of town. You go back to your own place. You just get out of here and stay out of here."

I wished I didn't have to fight him. I wasn't like Ernest, always losing his temper and wanting to fight. I didn't have a quick temper, and I didn't get much of a kick out of fighting. "You can't tell me where I can go. I have as much right to come here as you do."

"This is our place, Winchester. You got plenty of room at your own place, and you can stay there."

That was hard to answer. I had the whole estate to run around on—the pond, the fields, the stables. He couldn't go there—why should I be able to come into his part of town? But I couldn't admit that. "This is a public street," I said. "I have a right to walk on it."

He looked at Marie. "And we don't want you fooling around with our girls, either, Winchester."

That didn't sound like Benny, either. I had a feeling that a lot of those kinds of ideas were going around. I had a feeling that it wasn't just me that was the cause of it—it was the union and the strike that was coming and all of that. People were afraid of what the Winchester Mills were going to do, and it was making them hard and rough.

"Why is she supposed to be your girl, Briggs?"

Marie looked at me. "Chris—" she said.

"I'm giving you three to get out of here, Winchester. One—"

"Don't fight, you guys," Marie said. "Please don't fight." She looked scared, and I knew she was upset for being the cause of the trouble. "Don't fight."

"I told you, Winchester. I'm giving you three. Two—"

Suddenly Marie broke away and ran up the steps into the store. "Dad," she shouted. "Dad."

"Three," Briggs said. He put up his fists like a boxer, and I knew he expected me to fight like that. I put my hands up, too, and took a couple of steps forward. Then suddenly I put my head down and charged him. As I rushed him he got a good sock at the side of my head, but then I had him around the waist and was toppling him over backward.

"Hey," he shouted. "What the hell are you doing?" He gave me another slam on my head as we went down, but then we were on the ground and I was lying on top of him. He squirmed around under me, trying to get loose. I swung my fist, trying to hit him somewhere, but in that position I couldn't get in much of a punch. I swung again and caught him in the neck. He kept trying to swing at my face, but he wasn't in much of a position to hit, either.

Then I felt a sharp pull on the back of my shirt. Mr. Scalzo jerked me to my feet. "Cut it out, you guys," he shouted. "No more of this." I stood there panting and feeling sort of shaky. My face hurt where he'd hit me, and I wondered if I was bleeding. I didn't want to touch my skin, because I didn't want him to know he'd hurt me.

Briggs got up and began tucking in his shirt, like a fight was nothing to him. "You don't fight right, Winchester. Next time I'm going to fix you."

"Shut up, Benny," Mr. Scalzo said. "You go on home."

"I'm not getting out of here until Winchester does."

"Get out of here, Benny," Mr. Scalzo said. "I'll worry about Chris."

"I'm not going until—"

Mr. Scalzo jumped forward, his fist up. "I told you,

71

get out of here, Benny. I'll take care of Chris."

Just then Frankie Scalzo came around the corner of the building from the backyard, rubbing his eyes. "What's going on?"

Mr. Scalzo swung around and snapped his finger at Frankie. "You get, too, Frankie." He snapped his finger at Marie. "You, too, Marie. All of you. Get going. I want to talk to Chris." He stared around. Marie went back into the store. Frankie went over to Benny and said something, and then the two of them went off down the street together. It was the way I'd figured all along: Regardless of the fact that I was going with his sister, Frankie would side with Benny.

Mr. Scalzo stood there with his arms on his hips, waiting until everybody was gone. Then he turned and looked at me for a long minute. I didn't say anything. Finally he said in a soft voice, "Chris, you're a nice kid, and you're smart, and I hate like hell to do this. But you can't come around here anymore."

I was so surprised I couldn't think of anything to say. I just stood there with my mouth open, looking at him.

He looked back. "I'm sorry, Chris, but that's the way it is."

"But why? What did I do wrong?"

"Chris, there isn't any use in talking about it. You're a Winchester, and that's all there is to it. You aren't right for Marie."

I went on staring at him. "Are you saying I can't see Marie anymore?"

He paused a little to think. "No, I'm not saying that. Not yet. I got enough brains not to tell her to stay away

72

from you. She's got her own mind, and if I order her not to see you, it'd only make her want to do it all the more. I'm going to try to make her see it my way. In the meantime, I don't want you coming to the store." His voice wasn't so soft anymore.

"But why? Why?"

He looked away. "Chris, I don't think you realize how high feelings are running in town. I own a little store. I compete with supermarkets who can sell everything for ten, fifteen percent less than me. I depend on people who know I'll let them run up a bill when they're in trouble; I depend on people who like the friendliness of a little store. I built up a lot of goodwill in this town. I can't risk losing that. I'm not going to stop Marie from coming out to visit you or going to the state park with you. But I don't want you coming around to the store." He gave me a long look so I'd know he meant it, and then he turned and went into the store. I got on my bike, rode down to Main Street, and on out through town to where the farms and forests that belonged to the Winchesters began.

I was glad at least that I'd had the guts to take on Benny. I was proud of that. Maybe I might even have beaten him, if Mr. Scalzo hadn't pulled me off him. But that was the only thing I felt good about. For somehow, out of all of this, I'd become the enemy of everybody in town. Well, probably not everybody, but some people. They didn't want me around. What would happen the next time I went down to the Scalzos to see Marie? What would happen when I started school in the fall, which was only a month away? The way it looked, I

73

would have to fight somebody every day. It was pretty scary, knowing that a lot of people hated you, and wanted to hurt you if they could. Oh, how I wished that Ernest hadn't started all this. Oh, how I wished I'd stayed out of the whole thing in the first place.

I wondered about Teddy Melas. I figured I'd better call him pretty soon to find out what people were saying. Would he want to stop being friends now? What about Marie? I remembered her crying and saying she loved me. That made me smile. At least maybe it was still all right with Marie.

Riding along on my bike, I'd been so busy thinking and feeling things that I hadn't bothered to check out my face in a store window or something. But now I was coming up to the driveway of the estate. I stopped, set down my bike, and felt over my face. It was tender where Benny had hit me, especially on my left cheek and the left side of my forehead. But I didn't feel any cuts or dried blood. So I got back on the bike and rode into the driveway and up to the gatehouse.

Of course, the first thing that Mom said when she saw me was, "Chris, what's the matter?" She looked worried and grabbed hold of my chin so she could get a good look at my face. "What happened to you?"

"I got into a fight with Benny Briggs. I would have beat him, but Mr. Scalzo stopped it." I knew she wouldn't like the idea of a fight, but I felt proud about it, anyway.

"Did you start it again?"

"Mom, I didn't start the other fight. Ernest did. How come I always get blamed for everything?"

74

She let go of my chin. "Shush, shush, I'm not blaming you for anything. Tell me what happened."

"Benny came around to Scalzo's store to see Marie. I was out back talking to her, and when we came around the corner he was there. He told me to get out of there, I had my own place and didn't have any right to come to their part of town."

She sat down at the round oak table under the beaded lampshade. "He beat you up for coming into his part of town?"

"Mom, he didn't beat me up. If you want to know, I was on top of him when Mr. Scalzo broke it up."

She sighed. "All right. But that was the whole reason? It wasn't to get even for threatening him when you and Ernest caught him in the pond?"

I sat down at the table with her. "I don't know, Mom." I didn't feel so proud anymore. "Benny Briggs and those guys, they think I'm their enemy. And Mr. Scalzo, too. He told Marie that I wouldn't stick with her, I'd go off with my own people in the end. Who are my own people supposed to be? I don't want to be anybody's enemy."

"What about Marie? What does she say about it?"

I shook my head. "I don't know. I think she still likes me, but she's worried."

Mom ran her hand through my hair. "Poor Chris. You're caught right in the middle, aren't you?"

"Why do I have to be anybody's enemy? I'm not anybody's enemy."

She smiled a little sad smile. "Go look in the mirror, Chris."

CHAPTER 7

I didn't sleep too well that night. The left side of my face hurt, and when I accidentally turned over on that side, it woke me up. Besides, I kept worrying. Benny was going to go after me again when he got a chance, I was sure of that. The only way I could stop that was if I really beat the hell out of him, and I wasn't sure I could. On top of that, I didn't know if Teddy Melas would be my friend anymore. Oh, it worried me, and a couple of times I got up and sat on the edge of my bed, staring out into the moonlight falling on the fields, just feeling lousy. Finally it came to me that I should have a talk with Teddy. I should ask him flat out if he didn't want to do things with me anymore. Whatever happened after that, would happen. Once I decided that, I felt a little easier, and I went to sleep.

When I woke up there was a light rain falling. After breakfast I put on a jacket and baseball cap and went up to the stable. Durham said that we needed the rain. Besides, it would make the ground soft and easy to cultivate, so he sent me out with a hoe to weed the cutting garden. By the middle of the morning it was raining too hard for that. I went into the stable to wait until the rain eased up, and dried off as best as I could with some rags. I was trying to get my hair dry when Ernest came out to the stable. Usually in August Ernest wouldn't have been around. The whole family went up to their summer house in Bar Harbor, Maine, for the month. But Uncle Foster couldn't go, because of the negotiations with the workers, and he wanted Ernest to stay, too. Only Anne and her mother went.

Ernest said, "I was in Dad's office and I saw you through the window. I heard you had a fight with Briggs."

"Yeah," I said. I liked the idea that Ernest knew I'd had a fight.

"Is he a good fighter?"

"I don't know," I said. "He wanted to box, but I don't know anything about boxing, so I tackled him. He gave me a couple of good ones, but I gave him a couple, too, before Mr. Scalzo broke it up."

"I wish I had a chance to fight him," Ernest said. "I know how to box. I took it at school for a while."

"He's got long arms," I said.

"You have to get under them. You have to get inside and tie him up, and then work on his body."

"Well, I don't know anything about it," I said. "So I tackled him. I was on top of him when Mr. Scalzo broke it up."

"You should have got me to go with you, Chris. I'd have helped you. You stood up for me before. I'd have stood up for you."

He would have, too. I knew I could count on Ernest

77

to back me up. "What were you doing in your father's office?" I wasn't trying to change the subject. I was just curious, because usually Ernest didn't go in there unless Uncle Foster asked him to.

"Dad wanted to show me some stuff. He's teaching me about the negotiations."

"Teaching you?"

"He tells me what's going on. He says that someday we may be faced with another strike, and it's a good idea for me to get some experience of it now."

I sat down on a five-gallon can of liquid fertilizer. "Doesn't that scare you? I mean being in charge of stuff like that. Wouldn't you be worried about making a mistake?"

"That's why Dad's teaching me—so I won't make mistakes."

"But all the same, doesn't it worry you?"

"Sure it does. Sometimes when I'm down at the mills, I look around at all those buildings and all those people working there, and it scares me to think that someday I'm going to be running the whole thing. But then I tell myself not to worry—by that time I'll know a whole lot of stuff that I don't know now. That's why I always look at things. If I don't know how to do it, I can learn it, if I pay attention and work hard enough. You may not get it right the first time, but you can learn it if you keep at it."

I could see that was true about him. He took it for granted he could do anything he wanted to. It was the way he was brought up. If he wanted to be good at hockey, or riding, he could, if he stuck at it. And if he had to run a factory and deal with a strike, he could learn how to do it, too. Ernest made every team he went out for. It wasn't because he was always the best or the smartest kid, but because he was supposed to.

It was the way he was raised. He was *supposed* to be successful at things—it was sort of the family rule, the way in some families you're supposed to be religious, in some families you're supposed to be interested in books. In Ernest's family it didn't matter what you did, but you were supposed to be good at it. And I guess Ernest just didn't understand that most kids weren't like that.

But I could never explain anything like that to him, and I wasn't going to try. "Listen, is there going to be a strike?" I asked.

"The contract runs out on September first. We're negotiating with the union, but we're not getting anywhere. Dad thinks the union doesn't really want a settlement. He thinks they want a strike."

"Why would they want that? If they could get a settlement, wouldn't that be better than having everybody lose all that pay?"

"Dad says he thinks they want to show some muscle. He thinks they believe that if they come to a settlement too easily this time, we'll go right back at them for something more as soon as we can. He thinks they believe they need to strike the mills this time, so that next time we'll know they're not kidding."

I remembered what Uncle Foster had said about not

letting anyone erode your power. It was going to be the same kind of thing on both sides—nobody willing to back down for fear that the other side would think they were soft. I wondered: If Uncle Foster and Skipper brought me into the business and I became one of the top guys, would I be able to stand up to people, and take advantage of them when I had the chance? I could stand up to people if I had to. I'd stood up to Ernest sometimes, and I'd stood up to Benny Briggs, and other kids, too. But would I really like having to be tough all the time? I mean, it was one thing to stand up to people when you had to, but what would it be like always to be looking for the advantage over people? Suddenly I thought of something: Maybe that was why Dad went into the Peace Corps.

Just then Durham came into the stable. He looked at me and then turned and looked out at the rain again. "I don't guess we're going to get nothing done today," he said. "You might as well knock off, Chris. If it clears up this afternoon, we'll try again."

Ernest said, "Let's go up to my room and do something."

But I wanted to see Teddy Melas. Teddy was usually either cutting people's lawns or playing baseball, but with the rain I figured he would be home. I didn't want to tell Ernest I wanted to see Teddy instead of him. "I've got to do something for Mom," I said.

I went down to the gatehouse. Mom was working up at the big house, and the twins were at day care. I changed out of my wet clothes and fixed myself a cheese

80

sandwich. Then I put on my raincoat, got out my bike, and rode through the rain into town, and up the side street to Teddy's house. I chained my bike to the porch rail, and then I went up and knocked on their door. Teddy let me in. "Hi," he said.

The house was quiet, except for a soap opera going on the TV. "Nobody home?"

"Dad's around someplace." The Melases didn't have much more room than the Scalzos did—a living room, kitchen where they ate, and a back room with the washing machine and dryer. Upstairs there were two bedrooms, a bathroom, and the hall. Teddy and his two little brothers slept in one bedroom. There were two double-deckers in their bedroom. The brothers had one of them, and Teddy had the bottom of the other. Whenever I slept over, I took the top.

Teddy sat down on the old sofa with big flowers printed on it. I took off my jacket. I was wet, though, and didn't want to sit down. "Better give me some newspapers," I said.

"There's one on the table."

It was a copy of the *Everidge Ledger*. The headline said NO PROGRESS: STRIKE IMMINENT. I spread it out on the easy chair and sat down.

"I heard you had a fight with Benny Briggs."

Suddenly I realized that Teddy was looking kind of funny. He was frowning and looking here and there instead of straight at me. I got the feeling he wished I hadn't come. "I went to see Marie, and he came around while I was there."

81

"He's telling everybody he beat you up."

"He did like hell," I said. "I was on top of him when Mr. Scalzo broke it up."

"He said you jumped him from behind, so he really gave it to you."

"That's a fat lie," I said. "He was the one who started it. Ask Marie. She was standing right there. Where'd you get all this stuff, Teddy? Did Benny tell you that?"

"No." He went on looking funny. "Mr. Briggs told me. He came over this morning. He's outside in the garage with Dad."

"Mr. Briggs knows your dad?"

"He knows him from work. They both work in Supply. Sometimes they have a couple of beers together at the Wildcat after work."

That explained some of the things Mr. Melas had said the last time—how we should have let those guys swim, and the Winchesters could afford to pick up soda cans if people left them around. "Listen, Teddy," I said, "is everybody in town mad at me?"

"It's not just you, it's the Winchesters."

"But I don't run the mills. I don't live in the big house. I live in a little house like everybody else, and I have to work after school just like a lot of kids. Doesn't anybody realize that?"

"I don't guess so. All they know is that you're a Winchester."

I was beginning to feel sore. "But *you* know. Marie Scalzo knows—all the Scalzos know that I have to cut the grass and tend the gardens and shovel snow in the winter. You know I can't even be in the Babe Ruth League because I have to work for Durham. Why don't you tell them?"

Teddy looked away out the window. He didn't say anything.

"You could straighten them out, Teddy."

He went on looking out the window. "It wouldn't do any good," he said. "I'd never be able to convince them. They're so set against you, they'd think you'd bribed me or something. They'd just end up being mad at me."

I turned to see what he was looking at. Behind the house there was a little backyard where Mr. Melas had his rosebushes, to one side of the old garage. Mr. Melas and Mr. Briggs were just coming out from behind the garage. Mr. Briggs was carrying a shovel, and Mr. Melas had a pick. When they got to the cracked cement driveway that led to the garage from the street, Mr. Briggs stopped and banged the blade of the shovel on the cement a couple of times to knock dirt off it. Then they went into the garage. It seemed to me sort of strange that they would have been out there digging in the rain.

"Why won't it do any good?" I said.

"They all figure that when it comes down to it, you'll be with the Winchesters. They figure that someday you'll be one of the bosses."

It wasn't fair and I was getting sorer. "Who says I will? My dad didn't and maybe I wouldn't, either."

Teddy shrugged. "They wouldn't believe that anyone would give up all that money."

"My dad did."

"They've forgotten about that," he said.

"You could tell them, Teddy."

He looked out the window again, and I knew that he wasn't going to help me. It didn't matter what the truth of it was. He just didn't want anybody thinking he was on the side of the Winchesters. I felt hurt and cold. It was like being left on a desert island and watching while everybody else rowed away in a boat. I stood up. "If that's the way you feel I might as well go."

He jumped up, too. "Chris, don't be mad at me. I can't help it. I'll just be in trouble with everybody if I take your side too much. How can I do that?" He looked at me, with his hands out, like he was pleading with me to forgive him.

I stood there looking at him. I knew I would have to forgive him if we were ever going to be friends again, but I didn't want to. Look at the trouble I was in.

Then there was a banging and stamping at the back, and Mr. Melas and Mr. Briggs came into the house. They stopped in the kitchen to wash their hands. Teddy and I didn't say anything, but went on standing there. We heard them pop a couple of cans of beer, and then they came into the living room.

"What are you doing here, Chris?" Mr. Melas said.

"I came down to see Teddy. What's wrong with that?"

Mr. Melas looked at me for a minute. Then he said, "I'm sorry, Chris, but you can't come around here anymore."

Suddenly Mr. Briggs realized who I was. He was skinny like Benny, but not so tall. He was wearing a fisherman's hat and an old blue workshirt and jeans that had paint splotches and patches of mud at the knees, as if he'd been kneeling in wet dirt. He hadn't shaved. "You're the Winchester kid—the one who jumped my Benny from behind yesterday."

"I didn't jump him from behind," I shouted. "He's a liar."

Mr. Briggs took a couple of steps toward me. "Oh, no you don't, sonny boy. You don't call my son a liar." He reached out for me, to catch hold of my shirt. I jumped back.

Mr. Melas grabbed his arm and pulled him back. "Leave him alone, Harry. It isn't his fault." Then he looked at me. "I guess you'd better go, Chris."

I was shocked. Mr. Melas had taken me to baseball games at Fenway, he'd bought me hot dogs and soda and peanuts. I slept over there in Teddy's top bunk dozens of Saturday nights. I'd sat around in that living room watching TV with the family, I didn't know how many times, and I'd eaten dinner with them over and over. I stood there with my mouth open.

"Please, Chris," Mr. Melas said. "Just go before things get worse."

Harry Briggs shook his finger at me. "I want to tell you something, sonny boy. You think you're hot stuff because your name is Winchester, but you step out of line once more and you're going to get cut down to size."

"Be quiet, Harry," Mr. Melas said. "Now go, Chris."

CHAPTER 8

I rode home in the rain, feeling terrible. I was pretty near to crying. What hurt me worst was Mr. Melas kicking me out of their house. I could walk around that place blindfolded. I knew where everything was—where they kept the scissors, where Mr. Melas's tool kit was, all that stuff. Now I couldn't go there anymore. I wondered: When school started, would Teddy pretend he didn't know me?

When I got home Mom was sitting at the round oak table in the kitchen, with her glasses on and her shoe box full of accounts, paying the bills. She looked up. "Uncle Foster called a little while ago. He wants to see you. What were you doing out in this rain?"

"I went down to see Teddy. Mr. Melas kicked me out." I stood there looking down at her, waiting to see what she would say.

She looked up at me, thinking. Then she said, "Did he say why?"

"Benny Briggs's father was there. He made a grab for me, but Mr. Melas stopped him. Then Mr. Melas kicked me out."

She nodded. "Tempers are running high now, Chris. I think he'll get over it in time."

"I don't know," I said. "Teddy won't take my side, either."

"That's not Teddy, Chris. That's his dad. Don't blame Teddy. He has to do what his dad tells him. Just stay away from them for a while. It'll blow over." She took the phone bill out of the shoe box. "Better put on some dry clothes and go up to see Uncle Foster."

"What does he want?"

"It's probably about that fight you had with that boy."

"How did he find out about that?"

"I told him."

I was surprised. "You told him? Why did you tell him, Mom?"

"I had to," she said. "Uncle Foster is head of the family. He wants to know things like that. He'd have been angry at me if I hadn't and he'd found out."

"I still wish you hadn't. He's going to give me a talking-to."

She shrugged. "Chris, it's in your own best interest to listen to what Uncle Foster tells you."

But I wasn't sure of that. Maybe the best thing would be to get into some kind of social service work right here in Everidge, so people could see that I'd given up being a Winchester and was really on their side, spending my life helping them.

But I didn't want to say any of that, because I knew Mom would be against it, and she'd give me a talking-to also. "When am I supposed to go up to see Uncle Foster?"

"He said to come as soon as you got home."

I changed into dry clothes, combed my hair, put on my raincoat and baseball cap, and walked up the long driveway, under the arching sugar maples, up to the big house. I started to go around behind the house, so I could go in through the laundry room door, the way I usually did. Suddenly, for no reason I could think of, I decided to go in through the front door. I went up the wide granite steps to the big wood door with the great iron knocker and the diamond-shaped stained-glass window cut into it. I felt nervous, and I didn't know why. I just opened the door and walked into the front hall where the big staircase curved upward to the second floor. There was a painting of a ship by Winslow Homer on the wall. Casey was vacuuming the front hall.

"I hope you wiped your feet," she said.

I hadn't, but I said I had. Then I walked through the living room, with its huge Oriental rug forty feet long, old-fashioned sofas in red and gold fabric, and old oak tables with magazines neatly lined up on them, trying to pretend it was mine, just to see what that felt like. I went through the big dining room, which was mostly taken up with a long table with narrow legs that could seat twenty people, and our ancestors staring down at twenty empty chairs, still pretending. Then I went down the back hall to the office, as if I were going to my own office. I knocked on the door and stopped pretending.

"Yes?"

"It's Chris, Uncle Foster. Mom said you wanted to talk to me."

"Oh, yes, Chris. Come in." I went in. Uncle Foster

was sitting with his feet propped up on the wastebasket, reading a report. I sat down in one of the easy chairs, and looked around at the ship pictures and the old barometer hanging on the wall. Then I looked out into the rain falling on the driveway and the stable. It was empty; there was nobody in sight, no car parked there.

Finally Uncle Foster tossed the report onto his desk, took his feet off the wastebasket, and swung around to face me. "What's this story your mother tells me about a fight you had with a boy from town?"

"It wasn't much of a fight, Uncle Foster. Mr. Scalzo—" Then I realized he probably didn't have the faintest idea of who Mr. Scalzo was. "Somebody broke it up."

He squinted at me. "Your mother said it was the boy who started the trouble at the pond the other day."

"I guess he was sore about that." I didn't want to tell him any more about anything than I had to. All I wanted to do was stay out of the middle.

"What were you doing down there in that part of town, Chris?"

"I was visiting somebody I know."

"A girl?"

I blushed. "Yes."

He laughed. "Well, that's normal enough at your age. When I was about your age, maybe a little older, I used to sneak into town to see a girl I thought I was in love with."

"I wasn't sneaking. Mom knows I go there."

He stopped laughing and swiveled around so he was looking out at the rain. "I know this has been hard on you, Chris." He looked over his shoulder at me. "I suppose it's cost you some of your friends."

I thought about Teddy Melas. "My best friend was Teddy Melas. His dad won't let me go there anymore."

"I suppose he works at the mills — Mr. Melas."

"Yes. Mrs. Melas, too." Suddenly the realization of what it meant to have power flashed over me. Uncle Foster had the power to change the Melases' lives in a minute. He could suddenly promote Mr. Melas into a big job with double the salary, or he could fire him.

And I wondered what it felt like to Mr. Melas, knowing that some guy who lived in a big house on an estate, a guy who Mr. Melas couldn't even see, much less talk to, had all this power over him.

"And this girl — I won't ask you her name. Do her people work in the mills, too?"

"No. They own a little grocery store."

He gave me another quick look over his shoulder. "What was the fight really over, Chris? The girl?"

The truth was, I didn't really know what the fight had been over. Had it been over Marie? The pond? My coming into their part of town? What had it been about? "I don't know for sure." I still didn't want to tell him anything about it. If I told him too much, he might do something to somebody, and it would land back on me sooner or later. "I guess he was just sore about being chased out of the pond by Durham."

Uncle Foster was still looking out the window. "Your mother said that the boy told you to keep out of their part of town."

I wished she hadn't told him that. I wished she hadn't

said anything about it. "I guess he did. But he doesn't own the town. He can't tell me where to go."

Uncle Foster went on looking out the window, squinting one eye and then the next, thinking. Suddenly Durham came into sight, wearing waterproof boots, a slicker, and a rain hat. He walked on into the stable and disappeared. "Now you take Durham," Uncle Foster said. "He's valuable, because he likes his work and he takes pride in it. He's got a proprietary feeling about this place. He treats it as if it were his own, and he takes good care of it. He doesn't like to see anything amiss around here. I think he was personally affronted when he saw those kids in the pond the other day. When you find somebody who takes care of your business as if it were his own, you want to hang onto him. Durham's problem is that he goes too far with it sometimes. He figures he knows what needs to be done around here, and he doesn't like me giving directions. But I have to do it sometimes, just to remind him who's boss."

He was trying to get something across to me—about who was on which side. "I guess Durham was afraid those guys would give me and Ernest a beating."

"That was part of it," Uncle Foster said. "It's his job to see that things like that don't happen around here. But there's more to it than that. Durham's got his loyalties straight. He knows that if he does right by us, we'll do right by him. He knows that if he gets sick and can't work, he'll always be taken care of. That means a lot to people."

Suddenly Uncle Foster swiveled around to face me. "Chris, that boy was right. You don't have any business going into their part of town. We've got the mills and this place, and through our control of the bank, we hold mortgages on half the properties in town. It's only fair that we stay away from their turf."

"But Uncle Foster, my girlfriend lives down there."

He nodded. "Maybe you ought to stay away from their women, too."

That was exactly what Benny had said. I stared at Uncle Foster, unable to think of what to say.

"Look, Chris, suppose you were one of those kids and you got interested in a certain girl. And then along came somebody with money and good clothes and manners and all of that, and took your girl away. You'd feel pretty sore about it, wouldn't you?"

"But I don't have a lot of money and fancy clothes."

"I know you don't," he said. "But Benny Briggs doesn't see it that way. As he sees it, the girl can't help preferring you to him, because your family owns the mills and his family works in them."

I was surprised that he remembered Benny's name, and it came to me that he'd probably had somebody out investigating to find out who had poisoned poor Duchess. That made me pretty uneasy, because if he could pin it on Benny or his father, he was going to make it pretty hard for them. On top of it, I didn't like the idea that Marie liked me mainly because I was a Winchester. "But Marie knows I don't have any money."

"Yes, but surely she thinks that someday you might. Surely she knows that no matter what happens, you're not going to end up working in the mills or running a grocery store."

I'd never thought anything like that, and it bothered me a lot. Was it true? Did Marie believe that deep down I might end up rich? "I don't think she's after me for money. Her dad doesn't even want her to go around with me. He says like goes to like and I'll never stick with her."

"He's a smart man, Chris." He glanced at his watch. "Look, Chris, if you want to fool around with a girl like that, okay, that's natural for a kid your age. I did it myself, as I told you. I guess I was around fifteen, and Skipper put me to work on the assembly line in the Number Two mill, so I could get a feel of it. There was a really pretty girl working there, and I got interested in her and started dating her. When Skipper found out about it he said to me, 'Foster, go ahead and date that girl if you want. But tell me, what are you going to say to her ten years from now, when you're in charge and every time you go down to the mill you see her on the assembly line putting lock washers on a radio chassis? What are you going to say to her when she looks over her shoulder at you as you go by? Are you going to fire her, just so you won't have to face her?' "

I didn't say anything. Uncle Foster got up, came around the desk, and I got up out of the chair, too. He put his hand on my shoulder. "If you want to fool around with some girl like that, okay, I understand. But don't make it somebody so close to home." He patted my shoulder. "Think about it, Chris."

CHAPTER 9

I'd gotten an awful lot to worry about in one day. It seemed like everything I'd counted on in my life was falling apart. A week before I'd had a best friend, and a girlfriend, and a lot of other people who liked me. Now I didn't know what I had, or what was going to happen to my life. I didn't have any control over it anymore. Things were happening to me, and I couldn't find any way to stop them.

I walked back down to the gatehouse, thinking. The thing that bothered me the most was what Uncle Foster said about Marie. Did she really think that someday I would be rich and powerful? I'd never said anything like that to her. We never talked about the future very much, but anytime we did, I usually said that I'd probably go into social service, the way my dad did. I never said anything about going into the business, because it never occurred to me that I could. But maybe Marie had been smarter than I had about that. Maybe she'd realized all along that there was a good chance that Uncle Foster and Skipper would send me to college and take me into the business. Did she really dream about

94

marrying me and ending up living in the big house with lots of servants and five cars?

Maybe I knew less about Marie than I thought I did. Uncle Foster had called her "a girl like that." I knew what he meant—that she was the type of girl who would have sex with anyone. He thought I was going around with her for sex. Boy, was he wrong about that.

I decided to talk things over with Mom. I figured she might have a better idea of how Marie thought than Uncle Foster did. Marie had been around the gatehouse often enough. Mom knew her pretty well.

Because of the rain the twins had to stay inside all day, and they were cranky because they didn't have anything to do. There wasn't much room in the gatehouse, and they couldn't roar around on their bikes, or build big cities out of blocks the way Ernest and I did up at the big house when we were little. So I got out some cards and played Go Fish with them at the old oak table in the kitchen, while Mom cooked noodles and Swedish meatballs. After supper I washed the dishes, and then I put the twins in the bathtub and read *Winnie the Pooh* to them while they splashed around, supposedly washing themselves. The one thing that was big in the gatehouse was the bathtub. It was one of those old-fashioned ones with lion feet holding it off the ground. There was plenty of room in it for the twins.

Finally Mom put them to bed, and then she got herself a cup of tea and we sat at the oak table under the beaded lampshade. "So. What did Uncle Foster have to say, Chris?"

"I wish you hadn't told him so much about it, Mom. I wished you hadn't said anything to him about Marie."

"He has to know these things, Chris." She bent over her tea to blow on it, and her brown braids hung forward by her cheeks. I liked the idea that we both had dark hair and brown coloring. "I told you before, he expects to know things like that. He's head of the family."

"He isn't head of *our* family."

She straightened up from her tea and sipped it, and her braids fell back behind her head. "Chris, we don't really have a family separate from them. It's different in families like the Winchesters. It isn't the same as it is with people like the Scalzos. They can have a family separate from their relatives. But we can't, because Uncle Foster and Skipper control everything. If we have any hope of getting out of the gatehouse, we have to accept their authority."

It seemed to me that I was being given an awful lot of orders by the Winchesters. "I like living in the gatehouse."

Mom looked around and made a face. "Sure, it has some charm. But it's dark and it's too small for four people. How much longer do you think I can go on sleeping in a living room? Pretty soon you'll be wanting to have friends over and stay up late. Where am I going to go? Sleep in the car?"

I blushed. "Well, I can see that part."

Mom said, "I only took it because it was close to the big house. That was the reason."

I was surprised by that. "You mean we could have lived someplace else?"

"Of course, Chris. The Winchesters own property all over Everidge. We could have lived lots of places. In fact, Uncle Foster and Skipper didn't even think of putting us in the gatehouse. Nobody had lived in it for years. During World War II they needed everybody they could get to work in the mills. They were making electrical systems for tank engines, and they could sell everything they could make. So they cut down the house staff to a minimum, and they put the gatekeeper into the mills."

"They could order him to do that?"

"What choice did he have? So they closed the gatehouse and didn't reopen it after the war. When we came here I noticed that, and I told Uncle Foster that if he'd pay for the paint and so forth, I'd refurbish the place. I told him it would save on car expenses if I could walk to work at the big house. It suited him, because the gatehouse was just going to waste. But my real reason for wanting to live here was to be close to the family. I wanted you to grow up playing with Ernest and Anne. Why not? They're your cousins."

I was pretty surprised by that. Shocked, kind of, because Mom hadn't seemed to me the kind of person who would scheme something out like that. But I was curious as could be about it. "How come you wanted to be part of the Winchesters? I thought Dad was dead set against that."

She sat there looking at me for a minute, the light

from the beaded lampshade throwing a crooked shadow across her forehead. "You don't remember about coming here, do you?" she said. "You were pretty young."

"I was six."

She nodded. "Yes. Chris, I was pretty naive about this whole Winchester business when we came here. You remember, my dad was a steelworker. We didn't have much money when my dad was alive, and after he got killed in the car accident, we were right down to rock bottom, living in little rented apartments with cracked linoleum on the floors and cardboard in windows where the glass was broken and we couldn't afford to have it fixed." She wasn't looking at me anymore but was staring out into the shadows in the room, beyond the circle of light falling on the oak table.

"I joined the Peace Corps just to get away from all that. It was the only way I could think of. I wanted to get away from the smoke and the gray skies and the grease from the coal smoke that got onto everything. I wanted to get away from too many men coming home tired and filthy every night, with nothing for them to do but go down to the bar. So I joined the Peace Corps and got sent to Guatemala, and met your dad, and we got married. Of course he talked about his family, and how he had grown up, but he didn't really talk about it very much—he was too interested in our work, and that was what we talked about. I knew that the Winchesters owned a mill and had a lot of money, and a house with servants. But I didn't really understand what that meant. The only life I knew was the steelworker's life. And the life of an Indian peasant in the mountains of Guatemala. The Winchesters weren't real to me. They were like people out of a movie—interesting to hear about, but having nothing to do with me."

She looked directly at me. "Do you see what I mean, Chris? The Winchesters weren't real to me. They didn't exist. My idea of a big house with servants was one of those suburban houses that I'd seen outside of Pittsburgh. You know, a house with two bathrooms, and a maid who did the cleaning and cooking. I had a couple of friends from school who lived like that, and that's what I figured the Winchesters were like. And the mills—I had the same idea about them. Your dad said his people owned a factory where they made electronic equipment. The idea I had was of a big room in a loft where a couple of dozen people were putting together radios or something."

"You'd never met any of the Winchesters before? You'd never met Skipper or Uncle Foster?"

"No, none of them. It didn't make any sense for them to come down to Guatemala for the wedding, which was in that little chapel in the village that could hardly hold a dozen people. The idea was that when we got home leave, Dad would take me up here to meet them. But he was always so involved with some project that he kept postponing the leave, and we never came home at all the whole time."

She turned to look out into the shadows beyond the circle of light again. "We were down in Panama, you and me and the twins, who were only a couple of weeks old, when we heard that your dad had died. I sent a telegram to Skipper, and the next thing I knew, somebody from the State Department came and told us that he had arranged for a plane to take us back to the States the next morning. He came to get us in a limo, and we were the only people on the plane. That was when I began to get some inkling of what the Winchesters were all about. When we got to Kennedy Airport, there was a man from the State Department waiting for us. He pulled us out of the line at Customs and brought us in through a special door. He put us in another limo and we were driven straight up to Everidge. We drove up that driveway in that big car, me in old jeans and a khaki shirt, with two little babies and a little boy in torn jeans and sneakers with holes in the toes. Everything we owned was in two old, scratched suitcases, one of them with a rope around it to hold it closed. The butler met us at the drive and brought us up the steps through that huge front door, and I stood in that front hall under the Winslow Homer painting in my tattered clothes, holding two dirty babies, and you clinging to my leg. I stood there and watched as your uncle and aunt came down those wide stairs in their elegant clothes. And right then I said to myself, my children are going to have some of this, too. Their father grew up in this house, and they have a right to it. And as soon as I found out that the gatehouse was empty, I grabbed it."

I didn't say anything for a minute. This was a whole side of Mom I'd never seen, never knew about. It was kind of surprising to me. All along I'd figured she thought the same way about these things that Dad did—that you didn't want to spend your life trying to get one more dollar from somebody. But that wasn't so. She wanted us to get in on the Winchester thing, too.

"Mom, are you sore at Dad for giving all this up to go into the Peace Corps?"

She looked at me. "No. How could I be mad at him for that? If he hadn't gone to Guatemala, I'd never have met him. I'm not angry at your father for anything. He was a fine man—honest, dedicated, brave, generous. There was never a better man."

She looked back into the shadows outside the circle of light, and her face was sad. "But now he's dead, and he's been dead for eight years. It's been eight years since I heard the sound of his voice. I can't remember what it sounded like anymore." She looked at me again. "Can you remember him, Chris?"

I thought about it. "No," I said. "I remember a few things, like sitting on his lap while he talked with some of the Indians. And I remember once him putting me on a mule and holding me on while I got a ride. But most of what I remember is from the pictures in the album."

She drank some more tea. "I don't want you to forget him. I wish I'd taken some movies of him. I wish I even had a little bit of tape of his voice. But we didn't have electronic equipment—there wasn't any electricity up there, anyway. So I want you to remember always that your father was a wonderful man. You must always remember that." She was looking at me very straight

101

and serious. "But he's dead and gone. It's Uncle Foster who counts now."

I looked down at my hands in the light on the table. "Uncle Foster doesn't think the way Dad did. He thinks about his power a lot."

"Some people are like that," Mom said.

"I don't think I like it," I said slowly. "Why should I have power over other people?"

"The world has always been that way, Chris. Somebody has to be in charge."

"I can see that," I said. "But why should it be Uncle Foster?"

She shrugged and gave me a little smile. "No reason. That's just the way it is."

I was thinking about another thing, too. "Mom, when you married Dad, did you ever think that maybe someday he would quit doing social service work and go back to the family, and you'd be rich."

She hesitated. "I won't deny that it crossed my mind. But I would never have even hinted to him anything about it. Besides, I had no real idea of how rich and powerful the Winchesters were. Remember, I envisioned the whole thing on a much smaller scale." She paused. "Why do you ask?"

I blushed. "Uncle Foster said that Marie Scalzo liked me because she thought I might be rich someday."

Suddenly Mom laughed. "If she's got any brains she does. What girl in her right mind wouldn't want to catch a rich husband, especially a decent, good-looking boy like you."

I blushed some more. I wasn't all that decent, for one thing. "Why would she think that? I never told her that I might be rich. I never thought I would. And maybe I won't. Uncle Foster hasn't said anything about me going into the business."

"Chris, eight years ago, when I stood in that great hall in my shabby clothes with two dirty babies in my arms and a hot, sweaty little boy in torn sneakers clinging to my leg, I was Marie Scalzo. That was Marie Scalzo standing there. I come from the same kind of family Marie does. I grew up surrounded by people like the Scalzos. I know all about her. I know what's running through her head. She's dreaming about being Marie Winchester someday. She's dreaming about driving up to that little grocery store someday in a stretch limo and handing her dad a check for a hundred thousand dollars so he can buy a house in the suburbs. She's dreaming about standing on those steps up there at the top of the drive and saying, 'Good afternoon, Senator Smith, it's nice to see you again.' I know what she's dreaming. There are tens of thousands of kids all over the United States dreaming like that."

"Is that what you dreamed—that someday you would have part of the family's money?"

"No, Chris, I'm too smart for that now. I'm never going to get any of it. Oh, they'll take care of me, of course. I'm part of the family now, and no matter what happens, they'll see that I have a roof over my head and food to eat. But I'm Marie Scalzo. I didn't grow up in their world. I don't think the way they do. People like the Winchesters believe that they have a *right* to their privileges. They never question any of it. Oh, they give a lot of thought to their charities, of course. They give away more money in a year than most families see. But they never question any of it. People sometimes say that the Winchesters give to all those charities out of guilt, as a sop to their consciences. But they're wrong. The Winchesters don't feel guilty about having wealth and power. They give to charity simply because that's what people in their social class do. But that's not me, Chris. I know it, and they know it, and I'll never really be part of it. I'll always be the poor relative who helps to run the household. That's the beginning and the end of it. But I wanted you to have your chance."

"And the twins?"

"And the twins, of course. But they'll never have the chance you have, because you're six years ahead of them. It was you I was thinking of that afternoon when I stood in that entrance hall in those shabby jeans, watching your aunt and uncle come down those long stairs."

I thought about that for a minute. "Why would I have the chance, and not you?"

"For one thing, you're blood. I'm in the family by marriage. For another, you're male. The Winchesters are not feminists. For another, you're young and can be molded to their way. Remember what I told you before —they're always on the lookout for talent in the family they can make use of."

"But Mom, Uncle Foster has never said anything

about bringing me into the business."

"I can't promise you that he will," she said. "He hasn't said anything to me, and he won't. He'll simply assume that it's his decision, not mine. I just have a feeling in my bones." She stopped for a minute. "Did you know that Skipper's flying in from Switzerland?"

I hadn't seen my grandfather since Christmas. "He is?"

"It's because of the strike. He wants to be here, where he can be on top of things. We'll see what happens."

"Mom, suppose I don't want it. Suppose I'm like Dad, and decide to go into social service?"

She looked at me. "That's something you'll have to decide for yourself when the time comes. It's not a decision a fourteen-year-old boy should be making."

I thought some more. "Mom, do you think that if I married Marie, they wouldn't take me into the business?"

She shook her head. "They wouldn't like it very much. They'd expect you to marry somebody from your own social class, who had been trained to entertain, to manage a big household. They would want you to marry somebody who had grown up learning how to sit next to senators and even presidents and appear witty and charming and attractive. Do you think Marie could do that?"

"Mom, suppose I married Marie and went off and joined the Peace Corps or something."

"I don't think that's what Marie has in mind, Chris."

"I don't think you're right, Mom. I think she would do it."

She took hold of her chin and kind of nodded to herself. Then she said, "Why don't you bring Marie up here sometime and show her over the house? Sometime when nobody's around. Just to see how she reacts."

"Maybe I will," I said.

CHAPTER 10

It was the last week in August. The strike deadline was September 1, and a few days after that school would start. It wasn't very good timing. Half the kids' parents worked in the Winchester Mills, and by the first day of school they'd all be plenty sore at the Winchesters. There wasn't anything I could do about it. I had to go to school. All I could do was pray I could get them to understand that I wasn't as much of a Winchester as they thought.

As far as the strike went, I had pretty much given up trying to figure out the rights and wrongs of it. It was clear enough that there was plenty of foreign competition for the Winchester electronics division: You could see Japanese transistors and so forth in stores in Everidge. But were the mills really losing money? Was it all just a game to see if they could push wages down? If the union leaders couldn't prove it, I didn't see how I was going to be able to find out. I'd got one thing clear by now, though: The Winchesters had power and they were going to use it to the advantage of the family when they got a chance. When it came down to their own people, the Winchesters were as nice as they could be. For example, Uncle Foster's nurse, who took care of Dad and him when they were little, was pretty old now, and couldn't walk very well anymore. But Uncle Foster wouldn't put her in a nursing home, the way most people would. She was still living in her old room on the third floor: One of the maids carried her meals up on a tray, and Uncle Foster generally went up to chat with her for a few minutes every day. He always said, "She's spent all her life in this house, and she's going to die here."

But when it came down to the mill workers and other people in town, that was business and another matter altogether. It was a funny thing: The Winchesters were generous and kind to a lot of people. They hadn't had to take in Mom and me and the twins after Dad died, but they had. But they weren't generous and kind to everyone.

"Why should they be?" Mom said. "They can't take care of everybody in the world."

"Do you think they're trying to break the union?" I asked.

"I haven't any idea. If they are, we'll never know and neither will anyone else except Uncle Foster, Skipper, and one or two others. My advice to you, Chris, is to stay out of it. If any of your friends at school say anything to you, just tell them you don't know anything about it. Don't offer any ideas on the subject. Anything you say will be taken wrong." Of course, Mom didn't realize how tough it was going to be at school; none of them did.

To put it out of my mind, I concentrated on thinking about Marie. Did she really think I was going to end up living in the big house, and she might live there, too? I decided maybe I would do what Mom had suggested —take Marie up there and see what she said. It would be a good way to bring up the topic, anyway. Uncle Foster was at the mills practically night and day now; it would be easy to find a chance when nobody was around.

Then Skipper arrived from Switzerland, in order to be there for the strike. According to what Mom said, even though Uncle Foster ran the mills now, he looked up to Skipper and always consulted him on major things. Skipper had his own bedroom and living room on the second floor, but of course he ate with the family and generally used the living room downstairs to be with everybody. It had been his house once: He had been born there, right in that house, he had grown up there, and when his own dad, my great-grandfather, had died, it had become his and he had raised my dad and Uncle Foster there. He had a right to be there. He was tall and had white hair and carried a cane, but that was mostly for show, because he stood straight as an arrow and went riding for an hour every morning before breakfast. Everybody looked up to him, including Uncle Foster. We all called him Skipper, even Ernest and me.

I admit, I was kind of scared of him. I didn't know him very well, because he retired and moved to Switzerland a couple of years after we came to the gatehouse, and even though he came to visit four or five times a year, especially at Christmas, he usually had people to see in New York and Boston and Washington, and I never got to see him very much. So I didn't know him well, not the way Ernest did, who'd had him around all the time he was growing up. It made me nervous to talk to Skipper, for fear I would say something wrong.

The second day he was home from Switzerland he walked down to the gatehouse to see us. It was just after breakfast. I was washing the dishes and putting away the milk and cereal, and Mom was getting the twins dressed. We saw him pass by the window. "There's Skipper," I said.

"Oh, dear," Mom said. She quickly brushed back her hair with her fingers.

Skipper didn't knock—he just walked in. Mom went over and gave him a kiss on the cheek. "Hello, Skipper," she said. "It's nice to have you back."

"I wish I'd had a less troublesome reason for coming back," he said. He stood there just inside the door, looking around. "Hmm," he said after a minute. "I'd forgotten how small this place was. Can you manage all right?"

"We're all right for the moment," Mom said. "It's going to be a tight fit when the twins get bigger."

"Yes, I imagine it will."

"Would you like a cup of tea?" Mom said.

"I've just had my breakfast," he said. "But I'll sit for a minute." He sat down at the old oak table, his cane still in his hand. I noticed that the cane had the head of an eagle as the handle, an eagle with its beak wide

110

open. I started to clear away the rest of the cereal bowls, but he waved his hand at me. "Sit down, Christopher," he said. "It's been some time since we've had a talk."

I put the cereal bowls in the sink and sat down, feeling nervous. He sat there with one leg over the other, flicking the cane around a little, and looking at me. I noticed how blue his eyes were, like Ernest's. "How soon does school start for you, Christopher?"

"In about a week, Skipper." Ernest's private school didn't start for two weeks after that.

"And what grade are you going into?"

"I'm starting high school. The ninth grade."

"And do you like your school?"

Whoever liked school? "It's okay, I guess." He was making me more nervous with all his questions.

"I suppose you have a lot of friends at school."

Behind me Mom whispered something to the twins, and they slipped outside, to leave me alone with my grandfather. "Yes." I wondered if that was true. "Not so many as I would have if I lived closer to town, but I have friends."

"I see." He uncrossed his legs, put his cane straight up and down with his hands on top of it, and rested his chin on his hands, so he could stare straight into my face. "And Ernest—Ernest is one of your friends?"

"Sure. I guess Ernest is one of my best friends. Only he's away a lot. Teddy Melas is my best friend at school." That probably wasn't true anymore, either.

"Teddy Melas? Who's that? A boy from school?"

111

"Yes. We've been friends since first grade."

"And his people—who're they?" Skipper asked.

"His mom and dad work in the mills."

"I see." He took his chin off the head of his cane, sat up straight, looked away from me, and flicked the cane at a cornflake that was lying on the floor. "I understand from your uncle Foster that you have a girlfriend in town, too."

I blushed. I just wished everybody wasn't so interested in my girlfriend. "Yes," I said. "Her name's Marie Scalzo. She's very pretty and nice."

Skipper laughed. "I'm glad to hear that she's pretty. Nothing else will do for a Winchester. Your grandmother was a great beauty when she was young. After she came out in nineteen thirty-two, all the photographers wanted her to model for advertisements. But her father wouldn't allow it, of course. That was a different day. By the time Ernest's mother came along, young women were doing all kinds of things that would have been considered shocking in my time. Your aunt Ellen posed in garb her mother wouldn't have permitted the maids to wear. I think Anne takes after her grandmother—she has some of the same beauty, I think."

"My mother's pretty, too," I said.

He looked at me again. "Yes, I suppose she is," he said. "It's a different kind of beauty."

It wasn't as good a kind, was what he meant. Mom was dark and had dark eyes and dark brown hair, like me, and on Ernest's side they were all blond and light-skinned. "Her parents were Welsh," I said.

"I know," he said. Then he said, "Christopher, what

do you think of the idea of going away to a boarding school?"

"What?" I said. "Private school?" It was a complete shock. I'd never even thought that they might send me to a private school.

"You seem surprised," Skipper said.

"I thought—I mean Ernest—" I didn't know what to say.

He tapped the cane lightly on the floor and looked at me sharply. "There isn't any very good reason why you shouldn't have as good an education as Ernest, is there, Christopher?"

"No. There isn't."

"Good. I'm glad you feel that way. In retrospect, I can see that it's something we should have done sooner. We always intended something like this, if you showed promise. But you seemed to be doing well in school, and there didn't seem to be any rush about it."

I sat there feeling strange. So they had always had plans for me, provided I didn't mess things up some way. It was funny that they just took it for granted they could do what they wanted with me, without asking Mom. They were going to send me to college, and if I did well, bring me into the company. Someday, if everything went right, I would be rich. Someday I could have some of that power Uncle Foster talked about. I could see, easy enough, that if it ended up with Ernest running the company, I'd be right up at the top, not much below him. And maybe if his children went off into the Peace Corps, or moved to Paris to study art, my kids would take over when the time came.

Suddenly, all in a minute, the whole world had become different for me. It was like coming through a door into a beautiful garden and, at the end of the garden, a great mansion. The only trouble was, I didn't know if I wanted to step through that door into the garden. "Would I go to St. Paul's with Ernest?"

"I'm not sure," Skipper said. "We haven't got that far in our thinking. Perhaps it might be a better idea if you went someplace else. Ernest is established at St. Paul's and you'd just be following in his wake. It might be better for you to set your own course. Wakefield, perhaps."

That was the way the Winchesters were. They didn't do anything by chance, but looked at everything from all angles. "When would I start?"

"As soon as practicable, I should think," Skipper said.

"I'm not sure I could get into a private school. Besides, it's kind of late to apply."

Skipper laughed. "Christopher, we're not going to *ask* a school to admit you. We'll simply decide where you're to go, and when, and tell them." Then he stood up and flicked at the cornflake with his cane again. "I don't think you need bother working for Durham anymore. From now on I want you to concentrate on your studies. I'll have somebody make up a reading list. You can start on that until we settle the rest."

"Thank you, Skipper," I said. He walked out into the sunshine, and I followed him out, to be polite. My heart was beating fast, and I felt strange and different. The

114

twins were racing their bikes up and down the drive-way, and Mom was watching them. Skipper waved at them with his cane as he strolled by, and then went on up the driveway toward the house. I kept watching him as he walked through the shadows of the sugar maples. Finally I couldn't see him anymore.

When he was out of sight, Mom ran over to me. "What was it all about?"

I looked at her. "He wants me to go to private school. He says I don't have to work for Durham any-more, but should concentrate on my studies."

"Oh, Chris. How wonderful! I always said they had plans for you."

I stood there thinking. I knew I ought to be excited and happy, like a kid on Christmas morning. But there were too many parts to it that bothered me. "What if I decide I don't want to go into the business? What if I decide I want to go into social service, the way Dad did?"

She put her arm around my shoulder and kissed me on the side of my head. "Let's go inside and sit down."

We went in. She fixed herself a cup of tea, and we sat down at the oak table. The front door was open, and the sun streamed in through the screen door and fell in a patch on the floor. "Well," she said.

"I think they're trying to get me to break up with Marie," I said.

She blew on her tea, and then she sat there thinking. "No," she said finally. "It isn't just Marie. They see they've made a mistake. With all of this business about the strike, and the fight you and Ernest had with those boys at the pond, they've come to realize that you have a lot of friends in town."

I thought about that. "That's true. They're always asking about my friends."

"They see that you've developed some ties of loyalty there, and they realize they ought to have sent you to boarding school before. That's what it's about, Chris. They want you to make friends with what they think of as your social equals. So it isn't just Marie—it's everybody."

"I don't know why they're so worried," I said. "Nobody in town likes me anymore."

"That's another part of it," Mom said. "They want to get you out of town while the strike's on. They think it might be dangerous for you to be going to school here now."

"You mean they'd put me back in Everidge High when the strike's over?"

"Oh, no, they wouldn't do that," she said. "They have plans for you. They mean to see that you get a good education." She sipped at her tea. "Chris, it's a great opportunity for you, don't you see that?"

"Why do I have to take sides, Mom? Why can't I stay out of it? Why can't I be friends with everybody?"

She looked at me seriously. "Because you can't. There's going to be a strike and there are already hard feelings. In town they're going to say that if you're not with them, you're against them. Uncle Foster and Skipper and Ernest and the rest of the Winchesters are going to say the same. There isn't any way you can stay neutral, Chris. There isn't a chance of it."

"Maybe the strike won't last too long."

"It won't matter. There's going to be bitterness."

I didn't say anything. Then I said, "I'm getting tired of the Winchesters telling me what to do."

She shook her head. "Chris, you've got to understand that institutions run things. Large corporations, departments of government, big universities, publishing empires—these large institutions have the power, and they control the money. People who rise high in major institutions have the wealth and the power. The rest don't. If you're going to rise, you have to follow the rules of your institution, in your case the Winchester Mills."

"Suppose I don't want to do it? Suppose I want to do what Dad did?"

"Chris, in the end you have to do what will make you happiest in your life," she said. "I wouldn't want you to go into the company if it was going to make you miserable. No, if you're not comfortable with the idea, you shouldn't do it." She looked at me seriously. "But how are you going to know if you like it or not if you don't try it?"

CHAPTER 11

Skipper and Uncle Foster were very busy with the negotiations, and I didn't see much of them. But a couple of days after I'd had my talk with Skipper, Durham drove down to the gatehouse in the pickup truck and left off a stack of books—*Huckleberry Finn, Great Expectations, The Mill on the Floss,* stuff like that. They were already taking it for granted that I was going to private school, and they were going to be pretty shocked if I told them I didn't want to do it.

I hadn't talked to Marie for four or five days—not since Mr. Scalzo had told me not to come into the store anymore. That was a long time for us to go without talking to each other. I missed her. I missed talking to her, I missed seeing her, doing things together the way we did before. But I was nervous about calling her up, because of everything. Finally I decided to stop being nervous about it and I called her.

Luckily she answered herself. "It's Chris," I said.

"I thought you were mad at me," she said.

"Did your dad tell you he said I couldn't come around to the store anymore?"

"Yes," she said. "He wants me to break up with you."

I didn't say anything but sort of held my breath. She didn't say anything, either. I said, "Are you going to?"

She didn't say anything for another little bit, and then she said, "Chris, I can't talk," in a low voice.

"Mr. Melas won't let me go around there, either."

"He said that?"

"It turns out he's a big friend of Benny Briggs's father. Mr. Briggs was over there, and he was getting ready to punch me."

"Mr. Briggs was over at the Melases'? What was he doing there?"

Suddenly I remembered about the shovel and them digging behind the garage. I'd forgotten all about that, what with everything else I had on my mind. "I don't know. It was kind of funny. He and Mr. Melas were out in the rain, digging behind the garage."

"Maybe it had something to do with Mr. Melas's roses."

I decided I didn't want to think about that stuff anymore. "Probably. Listen, Marie, how about coming over tomorrow afternoon? There's something I want to talk to you about."

"Don't you have to work for Durham?"

"Not anymore. That's part of what I want to talk about."

So she said she'd see if she could take some time off from the store and come, and she did. She came up on her bike about noon, with her bathing suit and a package of Genoa salami. She was wearing pink shorts and a white blouse, and she looked as cute as could be. I was glad to see her.

"I brought some salami," she said.

"I told the twins we'd take them swimming." We went into the house. I got out a loaf of bread and we made some sandwiches. Then we changed into our bathing suits, collected the twins, and went over to the pond. Marie and I had a swim, and then we sat on the needles under the pines and ate the sandwiches while the twins splashed around near the bank where the water was shallow.

"So," she said, "what did you want to talk about? How come you don't have to work for Durham anymore?"

I was kind of nervous about how she would take it, but I had to tell her. "My grandfather wants me to go to a private school. He doesn't want me to go to Everidge High. That's why I don't have to work for Durham anymore. He wants me to concentrate on my studies, and he sent me a whole pile of books to read while I'm waiting to go to school."

She gave me a long look. "You mean you're going away to school, like your cousin?"

I looked back at her. "I didn't say I was going to go. I only said they want me to."

She sat with her legs crossed, looking at me. "I suppose your mom is all for it," she said.

"She wants me to do it." We looked at each other and I said, "I know what you're thinking. You're thinking I'm going to let you down, just like your dad said."

She looked down at the ground, picked up a handful

of pine needles, and threw them down again. "Like goes to like, my dad said."

"My dad didn't go to like," I said. "He married my mom, remember."

"But you're all Winchesters now," she said. "It doesn't matter what your dad did—you all turned back into Winchesters."

"Marie, please don't get sore. I didn't say I was going to do it. Let's just have a good time."

She didn't say anything. Then she looked out across the ponds, across the lawn beyond, to the big house. "What's it really like to be rich, Chris?"

I shook my head. "I don't know. We're not rich. We live in a little house, and Mom sleeps in the living room on a convertible. Your folks don't have to sleep in a living room on a convertible. Mom works and I work—at least I did—and we live like anybody else in town. We live like you and the Melases and the Briggses and everybody else."

"Yes, but you're part of it. You know what it's like."

I shook my head. "I don't think you ever really know what it's like to be rich just by watching it. I think you have to experience it yourself. I mean, you look at my cousin Ernest. He doesn't think about being rich very much. He just goes along like everybody else—you know, doing his homework and going out for teams and going to parties and so forth. But there's something about him that's different. The whole time he's been growing up he's known that he's *supposed* to be at the top. He's *supposed* to have command over other people. He doesn't think about it—he just knows it."

121

"What about you?" she said. "Aren't you supposed to be heading for the top, too, now? Aren't you supposed to be in command of other people? For instance me, and Teddy, and Benny Briggs. Someday you'll be able to take away our jobs, our homes, everything."

"Quit it, Marie," I said. "Don't start that. I'm not supposed to be in command of anybody yet. Maybe I never will be. I haven't decided to go to private school yet."

She didn't say anything. Then she said, "I'm sorry, Chris. But it seems like they're going to take you away from me. They don't think I'm good enough for them, do they?"

I didn't want to answer that. "Marie, even if I decided to go to private school, there's no guarantee that I would end up with a big job in the mills. You have to prove yourself first. You see what happened—the minute my grandfather decided to send me to private school, he gave me a huge stack of books to read. If I go to private school, I'll have to study hard and get good grades, and be on teams and all of that. If you're a Winchester, you're supposed to be good at things."

"What about your cousin's sister? What's her name? Does she have to prove herself?"

"Sure. But it's different. She's supposed to become cultivated."

"What's that?"

"Art and the ballet and museums and stuff. Her mother is always taking her down to New York on vacations. They stay at some big hotel and go to Carnegie Hall and the ballet and the theater. They shop for clothes and things. When she grows up, Anne is supposed to be able to have conversations with senators and famous writers and the presidents of corporations. She's supposed to know what's fashionable, and be stylish and put on dinner parties and all that."

"But suppose she doesn't want to go to the ballet and museums. Suppose she hates ballet and likes baseball or fishing. Suppose she wants to be a lawyer or something."

I thought about that for a minute. "Well, I guess if she really wanted to be a lawyer, she could. But I think the way she sees it is that she's training for being rich, and knowing famous people. They're always having the governor or somebody to lunch. My aunt and uncle go to the White House sometimes. Skipper knows the President—he knew him a long time ago, when he was just a congressman. I guess Anne figures it's worth it to go to the ballet and museums. It's sort of her job."

She went on looking at the big house. "Boy, what a feeling it must be to know that you're going to be rich when you're grown up."

Uncle Foster's Porsche came around the corner of the house from the stable. Ernest was with him. They went down the driveway and disappeared onto the road. I wondered who else was home. Skipper was bound to be at the mills, worrying about the strike. "Well, I don't know what it feels like. I never expected to have any of their money, at least up until now, and there's still a good chance I won't get it."

She looked at me curiously. "You mean, you'd give all that up?"

"My dad did."

She shook her head. "Not me," she said. "No way. If it was me I'd study ballet and go to art museums or whatever they wanted me to do. I'd do anything for the chance to be rich."

"What about your folks?"

"Oh, I'd buy them a big house in the suburbs and give them plenty of money so they wouldn't have to work anymore."

Was Mom right? Did Marie really hope that I'd be rich and marry her? Was that why she liked me? "Marie, what would you think if I told my grandfather I didn't want to go to private school? What would you think if I told him I just wanted to be an ordinary kid and grow up to be an ordinary person—you know, become a librarian or a scientist or get into social service of some kind?"

"What would I think?"

"Yes."

"I'd think you were crazy to do that. Why would you want to give up a chance to be rich? Who would want to do that?"

I looked down at the ground and picked up a handful of pine needles. I was beginning to think that Mom was right. Marie had got this dream in her head that maybe someday, somehow, she would be living in that big house. Sitting there, letting the pine needles run through my fingers, I had a lot of trouble fitting the Scalzos and the Winchesters together in my mind. Mr. Scalzo didn't have any idea of how Uncle Foster lived and what he thought, any more than Uncle Foster understood Mr.

Scalzo. Uncle Foster *thought* he understood the Scalzos, but he didn't. For example, he took it for granted that Marie would have sex with anybody who asked her, which was totally untrue. What would happen if I married Marie? Would they take her into the family? Or would they disown me? I was beginning to think something I'd never thought before: How would Marie fit in with the Winchesters? Could she learn to be part of a family like that? Now that we were talking about it, I could see that it wasn't just learning about the ballet and which kind of china to buy. The Winchesters had a whole way of thinking about things that Marie didn't understand. They didn't believe they were *lucky* to be rich and able to tell other people what to do—they thought that they had a *right* to it. In fact, now that I thought about it, I could see that the Winchesters believed that they and their friends were actually different from people like the Scalzos. They would never have admitted anything like that, but it was true.

"Marie," I said, "would you like to go up to the house and see what it's like in there?"

She gasped. "You mean we could do that?"

I was kind of nervous about the whole idea, because I didn't know what Uncle Foster or any of them would think of my bringing somebody up there. But it didn't seem likely that any of them were there. Besides, what could they say? If anybody caught us, I'd say that I wanted to show Marie the portraits of my ancestors, or something. They were my ancestors just as much as they were theirs, weren't they? "Sure," I said. "Only we better change out of our bathing suits."

We took the twins back to the gatehouse and left them with Mom, and changed into our clothes. Mom said, "Where are you two off to now?"

I gave her a look. "I'm going to take Marie up to the big house and show her around."

Mom nodded, but all she said was, "I see."

We walked up the driveway holding hands. I didn't say much, from being nervous, but Marie was excited and kept talking all the way about how funny it would feel to have servants and be able to tell them to do this and do that; be able to go to France whenever you wanted, just like that; and never to have to worry about money, ever.

We got to where the driveway circled in front of the big door, and I started to lead Marie around to the side entrance. But then I stopped. I wanted her to get the feeling of going in through the front door. We went up the main steps. I swung the door open, but Marie had turned around and was looking back down the driveway. I could tell she was pretending she was greeting some guests coming up the driveway.

We went into the entrance hall, with the big stairs and the painting by Winslow Homer. Marie stood there looking around. "Wow,' she said. "Does your aunt come sweeping down those stairs the way they do in the movies?"

"I guess so," I said. "If she feels like it." We went into the living room. Marie stood there looking around at the huge old-fashioned sofas, the tables with magazines neatly lined up on them, the big marble fireplace with the birch logs in it.

"Oh, boy," she said. Then she sat down on one of the sofas. She sat there kind of stiff, her back straight and one arm lying on the arm of the chair. "Jeeves, bring me some more tea," she said.

I laughed. "His name is Edwards."

"All right," she said. "Edwards, I think I'll have some ice cream and cake, too."

After that we went into the big dining room. She looked down the long table, ten chairs on each side. "Holy smoke," she said. She counted the chairs. "Twenty. Do they ever have twenty people over at once?"

"Sure," I said. "More than that, sometimes. When they have all the cousins for Thanksgiving and Christmas, they have to set up another table. You should see the cars parked out front. Nothing but Lincolns, Cadillacs, Rolls-Royces."

"How can they pass the food with a table that long?"

"They don't pass the food, Marie. Even if it's just them, the maids serve."

"You mean like in a restaurant?"

"No," I said. "They come around to each person with platters and dishes, and you help yourself. You're not supposed to start eating until the hostess is served, so she gets served first and puts her fork in her food as a sign she's started. That's so everybody can eat as soon as they get their food."

Suddenly Marie went to the end of the table, pulled out a chair, and sat. She looked up at the portraits on the walls. "Who are all those people?"

"My ancestors," I said. "That's my great-great-grandfather and my great-great-grandmother. That's my great-grandfather there."

"I don't even know who my great-grandfather was."

"Uncle Foster says that a gentleman knows the maiden names of his four great-grandmothers."

She went on looking. "Maybe someday your picture will be up there, too."

"Uncle Foster hasn't even got his picture up there yet."

"Oh," she said. She looked up the line of empty chairs and nodded to one of them. "Senator, how about some more beets?" she said.

I heard a noise. I looked up. Skipper was standing in the doorway, looking at us. I began to blush. Marie jumped up. "I was just showing her around," I said.

Skipper sort of flicked his cane a little. "Introduce me to your friend, Christopher."

I was still blushing. I knew that the gentleman should be presented to the lady, unless it was the President of the United States or something. I decided not to take a chance. "Skipper, this is Marie Scalzo."

Marie went up to my grandfather and shook hands. "Glad to meet you," she said.

"How do you do," my grandfather said. He looked at Marie for a minute. "Christopher told me you were pretty. I can see that he was right."

She blushed. "I don't know if I'm so pretty."

"And do you live in town?" Skipper said.

"You mean Everidge?"

"Yes."

"Yes, we live there. Up on Mechanic Street. My dad

has an Italian grocery store there. Maybe you've been there."

"I'm sorry, but I don't think I have. And do you have brothers and sisters?"

"I have a little sister. And my big brother, Frankie. He wants to quit school and go into stock car racing, but my dad won't let him. My day says he's got to finish high school."

"Your father's right," Skipper said. "You can't get anywhere without an education these days. It was easier in my day, but with the role computers are playing now, it's essential to have some training."

"Oh, I don't think Frankie would be any good at computers. If he just graduates, my dad will be happy."

"I see," Skipper said. "And you, Marie? What are your plans for yourself?"

Suddenly she frowned. "I'm going to go to college," she said. She'd never talked about going to college before—Mr. Scalzo would have trouble affording it.

"Oh?" Skipper said. He looked down at the floor for a moment and flicked the cane again. "And what do you plan to study, Marie?"

She licked her lips and took a quick look around the room. Then she looked back at Skipper. "I'm going to study art. And ballet," she said.

Skipper nodded, thinking. Then he said, "You might find it more useful to take a secretarial course. Or study accounting. Art and the dance are all well and good if you have the leisure for it, but for most people they're really not practical."

Marie frowned again and looked down. I wished

Skipper hadn't said anything like that. "Marie's pretty smart," I said.

Skipper waggled the cane. "I'm sure she is, Christopher. Still, it's just as well to be realistic."

I took a look at Marie. She was frowning and looking down, and her hands were clenched. "I can study art if I want," she said.

"Oh, of course," Skipper said. "Well, we all have things to do. It was nice to meet you, Marie." Then he turned, went out of the dining room, and down the hall to the office.

Marie stood there with her fists clenched, looking at me and frowning. "I'm not good enough for him, am I, Chris?" she said. "I beg your pardon, I mean Christopher."

"Don't get sore at me, Marie. I didn't say any of that."

"I can study art if I want to," she said. "I'm just as smart as your cousin. I can learn about ballet."

"Marie, calm down. He was just talking. He didn't mean anything by it." But I knew that he did.

"Oh, yes, he did," she said. "He meant I wasn't good enough for the Winchesters. He meant I wasn't good enough for you. Am I good enough for you, Christopher?"

"I never said you weren't, Marie. Stop making things up."

"Oh, I'm not making anything up. Dad was right. Like goes to like."

"Please, Marie." I took her hand. "We better go, anyway."

130

She jerked her hand away from mine. "Oh, I'll go all right. I know when I'm not wanted." She turned and marched off through the living room and out into the front hall. I followed after. She went through the big door, down the steps, and marched off down the drive-way, with me following along, not saying anything all the way down to the gatehouse. When we got there, Mom was in the kitchen. Marie just walked in, got her bathing suit, walked out, and picked up her bicycle. I stood there looking at her.

"Good-bye," she said. "Maybe I'll see you sometime, Chris." Then she rode away.

Mom came out and stared after her. "What's eating her?"

"She's just upset," I said.

"Did she hear anything about Benny Briggs's father? Was that it?"

"No," I said. "What happened to him?"

"They've arrested Harry Briggs for poisoning Duchess. They're throwing the book at the poor guy. They're going to destroy him if they can."

"Who's going to destroy him? The police?"

"Skipper and Uncle Foster. There's one thing you don't do in Everidge, and that's injure the Winchesters. Now they're going to destroy Briggs to teach the town a lesson."

CHAPTER 12

Ernest came rushing down to the gatehouse the next morning even before we were finished breakfast. He was all excited. He came charging in and said, "Chris, they're going to send you to Wakefield." He sat down at the oak table where we were eating cereal and toast. He took a piece of toast off the plate and began to spread it with the raspberry jam that Mom made every year. "They were talking about it this morning at breakfast, Dad and Skipper."

"Wakefield?" I said. "What kind of a place is it?"

"It's good," he said. "It's over by Worcester. You can drive over there from here in an hour or so. Who knows, we might end up going to college together, Chris."

"That's great, Ernest," Mom said. She looked at me. "Don't you think so, Chris?"

"Sure," I said. "It's terrific." But I wasn't sure. "Listen, Ernest, what about that guy who poisoned Duchess? Did he really do it?"

Ernest chewed his toast. "Sure he did. Dad had a private detective from Boston working on it. He gave the guy a fake job in the mill, supposedly as a busboy in the cafeteria picking up coffee cups and mopping around. A job like that gave him a good excuse to get around and listen to the people talk when they were on their coffee breaks. He heard a lot of talk—how Harry Briggs was going around saying he would get even with the Winchesters for what they did to Benny and all that."

"That doesn't prove anything," I said.

"Yeah, but then they found out that they had a lot of rat poison at Number Three mill. They use a lot of glue there, and it had been attracting rats. Seeing as Harry Briggs was in Supply, it would have been the easiest thing in the world for him to steal a whole lot of rat poison. The vet said it was rat poison that killed Duchess."

"But that still doesn't prove that Harry Briggs did it."

"Well, no. It doesn't exactly prove it. The police got a search warrant and went through the Briggses' house, but they didn't find anything."

Suddenly I knew what Harry Briggs and Mr. Melas had been burying behind the garage that day. "If they can't prove it, how can they arrest him?"

"That's the problem. They had to let him go for now. But we'll find something sooner or later."

But I knew where the proof was buried. I was a witness, and I could testify. I knew I ought to tell Skipper. Why should I protect the Briggses from anything? But I couldn't tell. "Maybe we shouldn't be so tough on Harry Briggs," I said. "I mean it was pretty bad to poison a dog that hadn't done anybody any harm, but it's not the same as hurting a human being."

"He's got it coming to him," Ernest said. "Dad says that when something like this happens, you've got to come down on the people who did it hard and fast. You can't let them get away with it, or they'll try something worse the next time."

I didn't want to talk about it anymore. There were too many things about it that were bothering me. Why did everybody have to be so tough all the time? What was Marie going to think about me now? So I changed the subject and we talked about Wakefield for a while, and whether I could make their baseball team, and after a while Ernest left. I took *Great Expectations* out into the field behind the gatehouse and sat up against a tree in the shade, trying to read. But I couldn't concentrate.

So I put a leaf in the book for a placemark, and went back into the gatehouse. "I'm going down to see Marie Scalzo," I told Mom.

She looked at me. "Chris, you'd be better off staying out of this. There's nothing you can do about it, and you'll only end up by antagonizing your uncle and your grandfather. This isn't the right time for that."

"I don't care," I said. "I want to find out if everybody thinks it's my fault. I don't want Marie blaming me for it."

"Chris, there isn't anything you can do about that. You're a Winchester, and they're going to blame the Winchesters."

I thought about that for a minute. I could see that it was true. "What's going to happen to Harry Briggs?"

"They'll probably be able to pin it on him. They can afford to spend anything they want on private detectives, and sooner or later they'll come up with something."

I thought about those two men digging in the rain behind the garage. "Maybe they won't," I said.

"Even if they don't, they can make life pretty hard for him around Everidge."

"How?"

"Well, the Winchesters own the bank, and the bank has mortgages on half the houses in town. A lot of the merchants owe them money, too. And of course everybody is economically dependent on the Winchester Mills. Half the adults in town work for the mills directly, and their paychecks support the other half. Look at the Scalzos—the entire family lives off that little store, and if people don't have paychecks to spend there, they'll go out of business. Think what the strike is going to mean to them. They'll have to let their regular customers charge for as long as the strike goes on—and how are they going to pay their own bills?"

That made it even worse. "Mom, I have to find out if Marie is blaming me for it. I'm going into town to see her."

Mom sighed. "Please be careful. There's an awful lot of animosity toward the Winchesters in town now."

"Maybe I'm not a Winchester after all," I said. I went out, got on my bike, and rode into town. All those woods I passed on the way didn't seem so pretty now. They seemed more like the outskirts of a fortress.

I got to Mechanic Street, went on up it, and locked my bike to the telephone pole outside the store. I was pretty nervous. They might already hate me. I went in.

Mr. Scalzo was waiting on a customer at the side counter. Marie was at the delicatessen cooler, slicing cheese for another customer. As I came in, both of them looked up to see who it was. Then quickly both looked back to what they were doing. I stood near the door and waited. Another customer came in, a woman I'd seen in the store before. She gave me a look, but she didn't say anything, either. Mr. Scalzo finished with his customer, took the money, and made change. The customer left. Mr. Scalzo looked at the new customer. "Hello there," he said, smiling. He began to take her order.

I went on standing there, feeling rotten, and watching Marie slice the cheese, slice some roast beef, fill a paper container with macaroni salad. She wrapped everything in a package, her hands twinkling swiftly along the way they always did. She didn't look at me, she didn't say anything at all, but did her work. Then she was finished. The customer stepped away from the counter. I started forward toward Marie. But before I'd taken two steps, she slipped away from the counter and disappeared into the back room. I stopped and looked at Mr. Scalzo. He was ringing up his customer's bill and handing her the change. Then she went out. The store was empty of customers.

Finally Mr. Scalzo looked at me. "You're not welcome in my store anymore, Chris."

I looked at him, feeling hot and prickly. "Mr. Scalzo, I didn't do anything. It isn't my fault that they're after Harry Briggs."

136

"It doesn't matter what you did or didn't do, Chris. Now please go."

I didn't move. "I want to talk to Marie."

"Marie doesn't want to talk to you. She doesn't want to see you anymore."

"You can't stop me from talking to her," I said.

"Oh, yes, I can, Chris. I'm not afraid of the Winchesters. If you try to see her, I'm going to beat the living daylights out of you. A man's a man, and I'll stand up for my family."

"I have a right to talk to her."

"You don't have a right to anything concerned with my family. You Winchesters think you own us all. Well, you don't, and I'm telling you right now, if you try to see my daughter I'm going to beat you within an inch of your life."

"Mr. Scalzo—"

He reached under the counter and came up with a cut-off baseball bat he kept there for when tough kids came in drunk, wanting beer. Carrying the baseball bat in one hand he came around the counter. "Get out of here, Chris."

His mouth was shut tight and his eyes were squinting, and I knew that he was going to hit me with the bat if I didn't leave. "All right," I said. "I'll go. But you can't stop me from seeing Marie."

"Chris, I'm warning you—"

I opened the door and went out. He slammed the door shut behind me. I stood out front, feeling shaky and angry. It was pretty scary to have somebody that sore at me. I looked up to the windows of the Scalzos' apartment over the store, in hopes of seeing Marie, but there was nobody there. I couldn't go on standing in front of the store: Sooner or later Mr. Scalzo would come out after me. So I unlocked my bike from the telephone pole and started to climb on. Just then I heard Marie's voice from somewhere around the corner of the house. "Chris, I'll meet you out at the state forest tonight, after supper." I didn't see her, I just heard her voice. It made me feel a lot better. I climbed on my bike and rode away.

There were a couple of state parks around, but I knew she meant the place where there was the field of wildflowers surrounded by woods, where we went a lot. If she was willing to go out there to meet me, I figured she wasn't too sore at me yet.

I didn't tell Mom what happened when I got home. I knew that if I did she'd try to keep me from going out that night. So I just said that I hadn't had a chance to talk to Marie, which was true, and had come home because there had been a lot of customers in the store, which was part true. I went back to sitting up against the tree, trying to read *Great Expectations*. But there were too many things whirling around in my mind, and around three o'clock I gave up and took the twins for a swim in the pond.

After supper I went out to get on my bike. Mom followed me out. "I don't want you going into town," she said. "I absolutely forbid it. It's too dangerous going down there at night, the way people feel."

"I'm not going into town," I said. "I'm going out to the state forest."

"At this time of day?"

"There's still plenty of light," I said. "I just feel like being by myself for a while." I didn't like lying to her, but I knew if I told her I was going to meet Marie, she wouldn't let me go.

"Don't be late. They way things are, I'll worry after it gets dark."

"I won't stay long," I said.

I rode on out there. I walked my bike into the woods a little way, then locked it to a tree. In the woods it was already pretty dark. I walked up the trail where we always went. There was a big oak tree at the edge of the field where we usually ate our picnics. Marie wasn't there yet. I sat down under the oak tree to wait. The sun had gone down behind the forest across the field, but there was a red streak across the sky there, and still plenty of light. Down below, in the field, it was darker, but there was enough light for me to make out the wildflowers nearest me. It was pretty calm and quiet there, and for the first time all day I felt peaceful. I'd spent a lot of time sitting under that tree with Marie. I wondered if this would be the last time.

I waited for nearly half an hour. Finally I heard footsteps on the trail. I stood up. Marie was coming along, in jeans and an old T-shirt. She looked very pretty to me. I gave her a hug. "Sorry I'm late," she said. "I told them I was going to a movie, but they were suspicious. When I was riding down Main Street I stopped and got

139

off my bike and pretended I was tying my shoe. I saw Frankie duck down behind a parked car. So I had to go into the movie and sit around for a while until I was sure he had gone home."

"Why are they blaming me for everything? I didn't want to kick Benny Briggs out of the pond in the first place. I'm not part of it in any way."

"Your family is really going to give it to Harry Briggs if they can."

"Look, Marie, he poisoned our dog." I wished I hadn't said "our."

"Maybe he had a right to poison the dog. If you're attacked by a dangerous dog, you've got a right to kill it."

"I already told you, Duchess didn't attack anybody."

"Benny Briggs said she did."

"That's a lie. I was there, Marie," I said.

"So was Benny."

I couldn't answer that. They were all determined to believe Benny's story, and they weren't going to change their minds. It wasn't fair to me, and it was making me kind of sore. But I didn't want to have a fight with Marie. "Well, all right," I said. "But Benny was in the wrong in the first place."

We were standing facing each other, very close, but not touching. It was getting darker, and we would have to go soon. For a minute neither of us said anything. Finally she said, "Chris, I can't see you anymore."

I looked at her face through the shadows. She looked very sad.

"How can you blame me for it?"

"I just can't see you."

I didn't say anything. I felt hurt and sad, too. "But why? Your dad doesn't have to know. We can come out here. Or I could meet you someplace in town." I grabbed her hand.

She let me take it. "Dad says if people knew I was seeing you, they'd stop trading at the store. They'd boycott it."

"Would they really? You didn't have anything to do with it. Would they really boycott the store?"

Her face was low and sad. She didn't look at me, but down at the ground, where we had trampled the long grass down. "Yes, they would. They'd do it. Everybody's sick of the Winchesters. The strike and everything, and then this thing with the Briggses. They hate the Winchesters. All right, if you want to say so, Benny shouldn't have gone swimming up there, and Harry Briggs shouldn't have poisoned that dog. But how do you think we feel, with you all living in that big house and owning five cars and the rest of us living down in town in our little apartments and lucky to own one car and dependent on the Winchesters for everything—our jobs, our money?"

I was feeling pushed around and sore again. "How do you think we live, Marie? Our house isn't any bigger than your apartment, and all we have is that beat-up, eight-year-old Chevvy."

"Come off it, Chris. You're going to private school now. You're going to be rich."

"Maybe I won't, Marie. Maybe I won't go into the business."

"You will," she said scornfully. "You will. And after that, you'll say good-bye to the rest of us."

"No, I won't. How can you say that?"

"They'll make you, Chris. Nobody has to tell me now. I saw the way your grandfather looked at me. I saw how he talked to me. All those questions, finding out who I was and what my folks did. When he finished questioning me like that, I felt like nothing. I'm not good enough for the Winchesters. I never should have started up with you. I was kidding myself all along."

I looked into her face. "Marie, if we ever got married, I'd make them accept you." But I wondered if I could.

"You couldn't make them. You couldn't make that old man do anything."

"I'd try."

"You'd try."

We stood facing each other, not saying anything. She reached up and kissed me. "Good-bye, Chris," she said.

"Marie—" Then I heard a noise and I looked around. Two guys were coming out of the shadows of the trees. "Who's that?" I said.

Marie turned. "Frankie," she said. "Oh, no."

I peered through the dark. They kept on coming toward us, and I saw that it was Frankie Scalzo and Benny Briggs.

"Run, Chris," Marie shouted. "Run."

CHAPTER 13

I didn't want to run. I wanted them to understand that I wasn't on anybody's side. I wanted to talk to them and get them to see that. "Listen, you guys," I said.

They walked up to me. "Get out of here, Marie," Frankie said. "Go home." They were standing on each side of me. There was no way I could run now, even if I decided to. Frankie was three years older than me, and a lot bigger.

"Frankie," Marie screamed, "for God's sake, don't do it. Chris didn't have anything to do with it."

"Shut up, Marie," Frankie said. "Go home."

I was good and scared. My heart was thumping and my throat was dry. But I was determined to talk to them. "Listen, you guys. Before you start anything, I just want to—"

Frankie slapped me hard across the face. My face stung and my eyes began to fill with tears. I shook my head so they wouldn't see the tears.

"Frankie, stop it," Marie screamed. "Stop it."

I shook my head again. "Frankie, listen to me a minute."

He turned and grabbed Marie by the arm and shook her. "Get out of here, Marie."

She jerked loose and started to swing her arm to hit

him, but he grabbed it and pushed her away. She went backward, and sat down. "I'm going to get the police," she shouted. "If you don't stop I'm going to get the police."

Frankie didn't pay any attention to her. He grabbed my arm and jerked me around so he was behind me. Then he put his arms through mine and pinioned me with my arms behind my back. "Okay, Benny," he said. "He's all yours. Give it to him good."

I began to twist and turn, grunting and sweating, but Frankie had me tight. Benny stepped forward and swung. I ducked my head and his fist caught me on the forehead. I kicked out at him and hit him in the legs. "Damn you," he said. He set himself and swung. This time he hit me directly in the middle of my face. I felt dizzy and shook my head and he hit me again. I tried to move my head from side to side, but the fists kept coming, and after a while I didn't know what was happening anymore.

I was lying on the ground on my face, and it was quiet. I hurt all over—my face, my head, my chest, my stomach, my arms. For a moment I lay there, trying to figure out what had happened. Then I remembered, and I realized that Frankie must have held me up a long time after I was out so Benny could go on slugging me. I lay there listening, to be sure they were gone. I didn't hear anything but peepers. I got up on my hands and knees. Everything hurt, and I wondered if I was bleeding inside. My nose was clogged and I couldn't breathe through it. I rested on my hands and knees for a minute. Then I knelt up and felt my face. It was wet with blood all over. I touched my nose. It hurt, and I figured it was broken. I dropped down to my hands and knees again, and twisted off a clump of grass. I tried to wipe my face with it, but it hurt too much and I threw it away. I remembered my handkerchief, and I wiped a little with that, but it still hurt.

I stood up. It made me dizzy to do that and I knelt down again, resting for a minute. I stood again, and this time I made it. I stood there praying that I wasn't hurt too badly, praying that I wasn't bleeding inside. Then I began to walk slowly along the trail to where I had left my bike. I could walk okay, although every step joggled something and hurt me. I touched my ribs on my left side. Something felt loose there. I was afraid that something might fall apart, and I walked as slow as I could to my bike. I unchained it and walked it out to the road.

Out there I decided against riding it. I didn't know what was broken inside me, and I didn't want to take a chance. I began going slowly along the road. About five minutes later I saw lights flashing down the road, and in half a minute a police car pulled up to me. A cop looked out. "You the Winchester kid?"

"Yes," I said. They told me to chain the bike to a tree. I did, and got in, and they drove me into town to Memorial Hospital, where they checked me out. My nose was broken, all right, and they'd torn some cartilage around my ribs. When I went to the bathroom to clean up a little, I was shocked to see myself in the mirror. There were cuts and bruises all over my face, my eyes were swollen like plums, and my nose was squashed.

They bandaged me up and then the cops drove me home to the gatehouse. "You can come down to the station house tomorrow and make a statement if you want. You can file charges. But my advice is for you to stay out of town. There's a lot of feeling against the Winchesters right now."

"What if I'm supposed to go to high school there?"

The cop who wasn't driving swiveled around to look at me. "The high school?"

"I might go there."

He shook his head. Then he said, "You better get your dad to send you someplace else for a while. The way they worked you over, they could just as well have killed you, son."

Of course, Mom almost went crazy when she saw me. She'd been worrying for about an hour and had been thinking of calling the police herself just about the time we drove up. The cop said, "We had the docs look him over. He's not bad hurt."

"What do you mean, he's not bad hurt? Look at him. Who did this to him?"

The cop shrugged. "Don't know. The way we get it, a bunch of kids were out at the state forest drinking beer and a fight broke out."

"He hasn't been drinking beer," Mom shouted. "Can you smell any beer?"

The cop shrugged. "You can press charges if you want, ma'am, but I'll be frank with you, I don't think you'll find anybody in this town who'll testify for you. They'd risk getting a dose of the same." He looked at her curiously. "You one of the Winchesters?"

"More than ever," she said. "Why do you ask?"

"I'm surprised you didn't have more sense than to let the kid go out at night alone, the way things are now."

"Believe me," she said, "he won't do it again."

Then the cops left. She made me take a hot bath to get some of the soreness out of my muscles. I nearly fell asleep in the tub. She knocked on the door. I got out, dried myself off, and put on my pajamas. Then I came out. "Mom, don't tell Uncle Foster and Skipper."

"Of course I'm going to tell them," she said.

"It'll just stir things up more." But that wasn't the real reason. I knew that they'd want me to testify against those guys. How could I testify against Marie's brother?

"Good lord, Chris. Just look at yourself—what am I going to tell them, you were hit by a truck?"

"We could think of something."

"They have to know," she said.

I went to bed and fell asleep pretty quick. But before I did, I wondered, just for a minute, if Marie would testify against Benny and Frankie.

In the morning, Uncle Foster and Skipper sent Durham down to the gatehouse in the limousine to bring me up to the big house. I was feeling very stiff and sore, and my nose hurt so much I couldn't touch it. But I could have walked up there. Durham said they didn't want me doing anything strenuous until they could get me looked after by specialists in Boston. The Winchesters gave a lot of money to the Everidge Memorial Hospital, but they always went to Boston when they were sick.

So I went on up to the big house and down to the office, with that antique desk, those pictures of ships, the old barometer. Uncle Foster was sitting behind his desk, and Skipper was in an easy chair with his cane across his lap. They didn't tell me to sit down, but let me stand there so they could look me over. Finally Skipper said, "They did a pretty good job on you, didn't they, Christopher." He pointed to the other easy chair with his cane. "Please sit down."

I sat. Uncle Foster leaned forward. "Who did it, Chris?"

"It was too dark for me to tell," I said. "They just jumped me in the dark and began hitting me. I went out pretty quick."

"But you must have some idea who it was."

"It was too dark to see. They came out of the woods. It was pretty dark in there. I guess they planned it that way."

They both looked at me. "You're sure?"

"Yes."

"What was it all about?" Uncle Foster said.

"Because of Benny Briggs's dad, I guess," I said. "And the strike. That, too, probably." I wanted them to know that they were partly responsible.

"Then it was the Briggs kid," Uncle Foster said.

"It might have been," I said. "I couldn't tell in the dark."

"You should have had better sense than to go down there at night alone," Skipper said.

"I've always gone there before," I said.

"Were you with the girl?" Skipper said. "The one you brought up to the house the other day?"

"Yes," I said.

Uncle Foster gave me a long look. "Chris, I warned you before to leave their girls alone. I warned you to stay away from them. You don't need any of that. Once you get to Wakefield you'll meet plenty of nice girls."

"She's a nice girl," I said.

Skipper nodded and began tapping his cane on the floor. "So that's what it was," he said. "It was because of the girl."

Suddenly I realized that it was part of it. Maybe a lot of it. The Scalzos were worried that Marie was impressed with me for being a Winchester, and might let me have sex with her; and that then I'd leave her. "It might have been," I said.

Skipper stopped tapping his cane and put it back over his lap again. "Christopher, you know perfectly well who those people were. It was the Briggs boy and some of his friends, wasn't it?"

Why was I sticking up for them against my own family, after what they did to me? "Yes, it was."

"The girl said she had a brother, didn't she? He was in on it, too, wasn't he?"

"Yes." I wondered what they would do to Benny and Frankie once they got them.

"How many altogether?"

"Just the two of them."

Uncle Foster swiveled around in his chair, put his feet on his wastebasket, and stared out the window onto the driveway. It was going to rain, and the wind was blowing a few dead leaves across the bluestone. "Chris, why are you trying to protect these people? I'm frankly puzzled." He gave me a look over his shoulder.

"It's because he's been going to school with those boys all those years," Skipper said. "We should have known better."

"Chris, what's the reason? These guys can't possibly be friends of yours now."

I didn't say anything, and they both looked at me. Then I said, "I just don't like to get anybody in trouble. I don't like them anymore, but I don't want them to get in trouble."

"But they've turned against you, Chris," Uncle Foster said. "Do you realize that they came close to killing you?"

"That's what the cop said."

Skipper tapped the end of his cane on the Oriental carpet again. "Are you telling us that you won't testify against those boys if you are called on to do it?"

I looked at him, and then at Uncle Foster, and then down at the floor. "No, I won't testify against them." I looked up at them. "I guess you won't send me to private school now."

Uncle Foster swiveled around to face me and waved his hand. "No, it isn't a question of that. But I'm still puzzled. I'd have thought you would want to see those guys get what was coming to them. I could understand if you got into a fight with the Briggs kid over the whole thing, or the girl's brother. But to be waylaid by two of them like that is something different altogether. That was vile and cowardly. It was unforgivable. You have every moral right to bring the police down on them."

I looked down at the Oriental rug, feeling rotten. Uncle Foster and Skipper would do everything for me, and I wouldn't cooperate with them. "I can't help it, Uncle Foster."

He breathed out a mouthful of air and looked at Skipper. "All I can say is that I'm baffled."

"It's simple," Skipper said. "He grew up with these people. He feels a loyalty to them."

But it wasn't that simple. Right there, at that moment, I had all the power of the Winchesters behind me. I could do an awful lot of harm to some people. I had the evidence against Benny's father and could get him in a lot of trouble. He'd lose his job, for sure. I didn't know exactly what would happen to Benny and Frankie if I testified against them, but at least a big fine and maybe a jail sentence for Frankie, because he was old enough. The disgrace would break Mr. Scalzo's heart. I had it in my power to wreck the lives of half a dozen people. And that was really why I wouldn't testify—I didn't want to use that power to destroy people.

Uncle Foster swiveled around to look out the window again. "Chris, let me ask you something. Suppose you were on the team negotiating with the union over the new contract. Where would your loyalties lie then?"

The phone rang. Uncle Foster picked it up. "Hello," he said. He listened for a minute, and then he said, "Thanks. Okay, thanks," and hung up. He looked at Skipper. "They've struck the mills. They're walking out right now."

It was a strange way to live. We couldn't really go anywhere. The family had always had most anything they needed delivered—like food, liquor, household supplies. They bought their clothes in Boston and New York—or Paris and London—and they had their own gasoline pump for the cars. So there wasn't much reason for leaving the estate. But it was strange for me. It was like living in a fort. I couldn't go to the movies or down to see Teddy Melas or Marie—all the things I used to do. The life that I had lived for eight years was over and done with. I knew that now. I wouldn't see Teddy again for years, and maybe never.

And probably not Marie, either. I was going to miss her a lot. I was beginning to miss her already. I kept getting pictures of her in my head—the way she had of moving her hands when she talked, the way she liked to swim on her back, the way she had of looking right at you when she talked. One day I went down to the gatehouse, rummaged around in my old dresser drawer, and found a picture she had given me a long time ago. I kept the picture in my wallet and I took it out and looked at it a lot.

Mom was busy most of the time. Uncle Foster and Skipper had their hands full with the strike, and Mom had to take care of a lot of the family business by herself—check the bills, see that the servants got paid, take care of the banking. When she went into town to the bank, a state trooper drove her in and went into the bank with her.

It was a funny thing: Since I'd got beaten up and the strike had started, we seemed to belong to the family

153

more. I could tell that Skipper and Uncle Foster were depending on Mom more, and I got the feeling that they were probably going to do something for her—get her a better place to live and more money to go along with it. As for me, it was the first time that I'd ever been in on something that Ernest was out of. Now it was me who listened to Skipper, Uncle Foster, and Aunt Ellen talk over meals, when they happened to be around for them. I knew a whole lot more about what was going on than Ernest did.

That was how I found out that Frankie Scalzo had been arrested. It was about ten days after I'd got beaten up and the strike had started. My nose was a lot better, and I'd be going away soon. The strike hadn't yet become violent, but it was going that way. There were long picket lines around the factory, and whenever management people went in and out, the workers jeered and shouted. A few times they had thrown stuff, too—mostly eggs and tomatoes, but some stones, too. When that happened, the state police had charged the pickets, and a couple of people had got hurt. The workers were angry, and they were getting angrier. The strike was costing them a half million dollars a day in pay, the *Everidge Ledger* said.

"They won't last four months," Uncle Foster said. "Wait until the cold weather hits and they're out there on that picket line in the freezing rain and snow. Wait until December when the oil company runs out of money because nobody's paid them, and they can't get fuel oil anymore. Wait until they have to close the schools because nobody's paid their taxes and the teachers are out of work. They'll cave in. We haven't had a strike up here for two generations. These people don't know what it's like."

Anyway, one night at dinner Uncle Foster said, "Chris, I thought you'd want to know that the Scalzo boy has been arrested."

"Arrested?"

"He and the Briggs boy."

"For what they did to me?"

"No, don't worry about that, Chris. It has nothing to do with that. They were caught inside one of the mills. They were trying to start a fire. They were caught with two five-gallon cans of gasoline, newspaper, matches. They were caught red-handed. That's attempted arson. It's a serious offense. The Briggs boy is underage and he can't be charged—he'll go before a juvenile court. But Scalzo is seventeen. The chances are pretty good he'll end up in the penitentiary."

It was going to be awful for the Scalzos if Frankie went to jail. It would break their hearts. Mr. Scalzo had worked day and night to build up his business for Frankie to take over. All that would be ruined. Sure, I didn't feel much sorry for Frankie, not after he'd given me that beating. But I felt sorry for the rest of them, especially Mr. Scalzo. His family meant everything to him.

"It's surprising to me that Frankie would do something like that, Uncle Foster. He never seemed like a criminal to me."

Uncle Foster gave me a look. "Feelings are running high in town. You ought to know that as well as any-

155

body. When you get that kind of situation, people do all sorts of things they wouldn't usually do. You saw those pictures in the paper the other day—women throwing stones at the oil truck going into the plant. Those are ordinary housewives. A lot of them are mothers. They've probably never done anything violent in their lives. But feelings are high now."

The whole thing bothered me a lot. I still had the feeling that it was my fault, that somehow it had to do with what Frankie did to me. There was something about it that didn't make sense. Frankie was sort of tough, but he was pretty lazy, too. He wasn't the type of guy who would get up a scheme to burn down the mills by himself.

There was a story about it in the *Ledger* the next day. It wasn't much of a story, only three or four paragraphs long. It said that Frankie and Benny had been caught in the Number Three mill with incendiary materials. They claimed they had been framed. Somebody had paid them money to take the five-gallon cans into the yard, they said. They'd been told it was cleaning fluid, not gasoline, they claimed. But according to the prosecutor, Scalzo and Briggs were known to bear a grievance against the Winchester family and had a motive for the act.

I knew Frankie. You could take him in with a story like that, if you gave him some money. It seemed like too much of a coincidence that it just happened to be the two guys who'd beaten me up who got caught. Frankie and Benny weren't pals, especially. Just to begin with, Frankie was a couple of years older than Benny. But there was the other side to it: The prosecutor was right; Frankie and Benny sure had a grievance against the Winchesters. I wished I knew the truth: I wished there was somebody I could ask about it. But there wasn't, and I'd be going away to school soon, anyway. I'd been back to Boston and the doctor had taken the bandage off my nose. He said I could go, and Mom had taken me into Boston and bought me a lot of new clothes, which Uncle Foster paid for. That was one of the advantages of being a Winchester: They weren't going to let me go around looking poor.

When I woke the next morning, it was pouring rain. I was pretty bored by that time, and rain would make it worse. When the weather was good I could always take the twins swimming or just walk around outside when I got tired of reading. But in the rain I was stuck. I would be glad when I could finally go to school.

So I spent the morning reading, and after lunch I played Go Fish with the twins, which wasn't much help with the boredom. Then around three o'clock one of the maids came up and said there was a state trooper downstairs who wanted to see me.

I went down. The trooper was standing in the hall in a big slicker, dripping water onto the rubber mat they put down when it rained. "There's a girl down by the gatehouse who wants to see you."

My heart jumped. It had to be Marie. I wanted to see her, and it made me glad that she had come to see me. "I'll go right down," I said.

"Listen, you better go with me. It might be a trap."

But I didn't want to talk to Marie in front of a state trooper. "I'll be all right," I said.

Just then Mom appeared. "Marie's down at the gatehouse," I said.

Mom shook her head. "You're not going," she said. "You're going to stay right here, Chris. I'm not taking any more chances with you."

"Mom, I'm going. You can't stop me."

She looked at the trooper. "Go on back down there and tell her Chris isn't here. Tell her he's gone away to school."

"I think that's a good idea, ma'am." Mom had already taken on some of the power of the Winchesters; now she could give orders to state troopers.

"Damn you, Mom, I'm going," I shouted.

"No, you're not, Chris. I let you go once when I shouldn't have, and I'm not doing it again."

The trooper went out the door and shut it. I turned to run. Mom grabbed hold of the front of my shirt. "Chris, it's a trap."

"No, it isn't," I shouted. "Marie wouldn't trap me. I'm going." She hung onto my shirt, but I was stronger than she was, and I broke loose. I slammed open the front door and ran out into the rain.

"Chris," she shouted. "Come back." But I went on running. The police car was already halfway down the drive, and going much faster than I could go. I ran on. I figured that Mom would call down to the gatehouse to have them hold me there. I swerved off the driveway into the field. The hay was soaked, and my shoes and pants got wet through in a minute. I skirted around the pond and then through the pine trees toward the road. By now I was totally wet. I didn't care. I went on running, and in a minute I came out on the road, in the direction of town from the gatehouse. I knelt down there and looked out. Marie was already past me, headed toward town on her bike. She was wearing a red raincoat and red rain hat, and riding slowly. "Marie," I shouted.

She didn't hear me. I began to run down the road after her. "Marie," I shouted again.

This time she turned her head. When she saw it was me she stopped, slipped off the bike, and stood there waiting for me. I ran up. She laid down the bike. "The cop said you'd already gone to school."

"They didn't want me to come. They were afraid you were setting a trap for me." I reached out to catch hold of her hand.

She pulled her hand away. "Don't, Chris." She gave me a cool, steady look. "I see Benny broke your nose. He said he thought he did. You won't be so good-looking anymore."

"Marie, I didn't have anything to do with getting Frankie arrested. What could I do about it?"

"You could ask them to let him go. They'll let him go if you ask."

"Marie, they wanted me to testify about Frankie and Benny after they beat me up. I told them I wouldn't. I refused to do it. You can't blame me for it."

The rain was pouring down on us pretty hard. It was running down our faces and under our collars. "You're a Winchester now," she said. "I can blame you for everything. You're trying to ruin us."

"What do you mean, us?"

"Us. Everybody in town. You'll do any kind of dirty trick to hurt us for no reason. You think you're too good for us now. Well, you're not. You're the scum of the earth, all of you."

She hated me, and I could see there was no hope of changing that, maybe ever. I felt just terrible, hurting inside worse than when Benny and Frankie had hurt me. I wanted to put my arms around her, to hug her. It was bad enough to know that we couldn't see each other. But it was far worse to realize that she hated me. "Marie, I didn't do any of those things."

"It doesn't matter who did them. You're all on the same side now. You were too good for me, and now you won't stop them from destroying us."

I took a deep breath to try to calm myself down. "Do you think that Uncle Foster and Skipper framed them?"

She spit into the grass. "Of course they framed them. This guy told Frankie he was supposed to make a delivery of cleaning fluid, but he was afraid of the strikers and didn't want to cross the picket line. He gave Frankie and Benny twenty bucks each to go in there. He told them where there was a back gate that was unlocked. As soon as they came through the gate, the cops nabbed them. They were lying in wait."

I stood there thinking about it. I didn't want to believe it. I hoped it wasn't true. "Are you sure that's right? Are you sure it wasn't just a story Frankie made up after he was caught?"

She gave me a hard look. "Frankie couldn't make up a story like that."

I wanted to put my arms around her so badly I could hardly stop myself. My hair was soaked and the water was running down the back of my neck onto my skin. "Marie, if you believe that, why did you come up here to see me?"

"I came up to beg, Chris. I came up to beg you to ask that old man to let Frankie go."

"He isn't the police. He can't do that."

"Yes, he can," she said. "Around here the Winchesters can do anything they want."

That was true—at least it was true that Skipper could get Frankie off if he wanted. "It wouldn't do any good for me to ask. They don't do what I ask."

"You could try. You could beg them."

I thought about it. "Marie, I wish I could do something. I didn't want them to get Frankie in trouble."

She looked at me, her face soaked with rain, the water running down her cheeks and dripping off her chin. "Chris, the reason why I came up here was to tell you I'd have sex with you if you'll ask them to let Frankie go."

I was shocked. I stared at her. "You'd have sex with me? But where?"

"Here. Right now. We could go over there into the pine trees." She began to unbutton her raincoat. "Here," she said. She reached in under the raincoat to unbutton her blouse. "You can feel me up if you want. You can do anything you want."

I wanted to. Even with everything, I wanted to. I

closed my eyes, feeling weak. "No," I said. "No."

"Why not, all of a sudden? You always wanted to before."

I kept my eyes closed. "I want to, but I'm not going to."

She took my hand, pulled it toward her, and pushed it under her blouse. "No," I said. I pulled my hand out of her grip.

I heard the sound of a car engine in the distance. I opened my eyes and looked. The police car was pulling out of the driveway. It headed toward us. Marie had her blouse totally undone. She had nothing on underneath. "No," I said.

The police car came up, and the trooper leaned out. "Everything okay? No problems?"

"No problems," I said. I turned and trotted across the road, into the pines, heading toward the big house. It was all ruined—everything was ruined, and I began to cry.

CHAPTER 15

Mom was standing in the front door, out of the rain, watching me run up the driveway. I shook myself to stop crying. I reached the steps and started up. She said, "That was a crazy thing to do, Chris. It might have been a trap."

"It wasn't a trap," I said. I reached the top step. "Mom, did they frame Benny and Frankie?"

"Let's go in out of the rain."

"I want an answer."

"I'll give you an answer. But first come in and dry off." I came in. We went upstairs to where our rooms were. I took a shower and changed into dry clothes, and then sat in Mom's bedroom. She had a bottle of sherry in her closet, and she poured some into a glass on her bedside table.

"What did Marie want?"

"She said she'd have sex with me if I'd beg Uncle Foster and Skipper to let Frankie off."

Her eyes got wide and she didn't say anything for a minute. Then she said, "You never had sex with her before?"

"No," I said. "She didn't believe in it."

163

"I was never sure," Mom said. She took a sip of her sherry.

"Mom, did they frame those guys?"

She waited a minute. Then she said, "Chris, we can't remake the world. Your grandfather and your uncle are in a very tough fight right now with the people in the town. Sometimes when there's a battle like this, people feel they have to do things they might not do at other times."

"So they did it."

She sipped at her sherry again. "Nobody ever told me that in so many words."

"And you think it's right."

"No, I don't," she said. "But what Benny Briggs and Frankie Scalzo did to you wasn't right, either."

"Two wrongs don't make a right."

"That's a nice saying, Chris. It isn't the way things are. You're one of the Winchesters. They aren't going to let something like that happen to a Winchester."

I didn't say anything. Whatever reasons Skipper and Uncle Foster had for what they did, I couldn't accept it. They were going to ruin a lot of people's lives just to prove that they could. I knew what I had to do. I didn't know if it was right or wrong, but I was going to do it. I got up and started out of the room.

"Where are you going now, Chris?"

"I'm going to talk to them."

"Who?"

"You know." I went out of the room, down the stairs, and along the corridor to the back of the house. I knocked on the office door.

"What is it?" Uncle Foster said.

"It's Chris," I said.

"Chris, we're pretty busy," he said through the door.

"I have to talk about it now." I guess Uncle Foster could hear in my voice that it was serious, for he told me to come in.

Uncle Foster was sitting at his desk as usual, with his feet up on his wastebasket, looking out into the rain pouring down on the driveway, on the slate roof of the barn, on the fields beyond. My grandfather was in the easy chair with his cane across his knees. I didn't sit down but stood near the door.

"What is it, Christopher?" Skipper asked.

"Did you frame Benny Briggs and Frankie Scalzo?"

Uncle Foster swung his feet off the wastebasket and swiveled around to face me. "Chris, I think—"

"Of course we framed them," Skipper said. "Or, to be completely accurate, we paid somebody to do it for us."

"You got some guy to give them twenty dollars to—"

Skipper held up his hand. "Let's not get into the details. I don't think that's the point."

I looked from one to the other. "But why? Why did you have to do it?"

"I should think you of all people would understand that," Skipper said. I could see that Uncle Foster was leaving it up to Skipper.

"I said I wouldn't testify against them."

"Yes. That's why we had to take another route."

"But why? Couldn't you have just forgotten about it? It's going to be terrible for the Scalzos. It's going to be just awful for them if Frankie goes to jail."

"No doubt it will," Skipper said. He put the end of his cane on the floor, cupped his hands over the handle, and rested his chin on his hands. "But then it was pretty awful for you to endure that beating. Suppose they'd given you some kind of permanent injury, which they might easily have done. That would have been pretty awful, too."

"But they didn't hurt me that bad."

Skipper shook his head. "Christopher, you can't let people who injure you like that go unpunished. You have to strike hard and fast. You have to teach them a lesson they'll never forget." He sat up and flicked the cane at a speck in the Oriental carpet. "Don't think for a minute that we did it to avenge your honor, or pride, or something like that. What you feel about it is irrelevant. We just could not permit anybody to do something like that to one of us. Nobody touches our people with impunity. Nobody." He tapped the cane on the floor.

"I was the one who got beat up," I said. "Why wasn't it up to me to decide about it?"

"Christopher, if you show signs of weakness, people will start nibbling away at your power, and soon enough you won't have it anymore."

"But maybe we shouldn't have all this power. Maybe we should share it."

"Quite possibly," Skipper said. "Many things are possible, and I'm sure that when you go to college and study philosophy, as I hope you'll do, you'll look at all of these questions seriously. But as for me, for whatever

166

reasons, we have the power. And I can see no point in surrendering it to somebody else who probably will do no better with it than we have, and might do worse."

What he was saying was beginning to confuse me, and I decided I'd better not try to argue with him. "Skipper," I said, "I'm begging you to let those guys off."

"Winchesters don't beg, Christopher."

"All right. I'm asking it."

Now Uncle Foster began tapping a pencil on his desk very fast. "We can't do that, Chris," he said. "We can't show weakness now. Not with the strike on. It would be fatal. We've got to show them we're implacable, unshakable."

"Hold on a minute, Foster," Skipper said. "Just think what the boy is going through. He's had to change a whole set of loyalties almost overnight." He looked at me. "Christopher, what if we don't let them off, as you put it?"

I took a deep breath. "If you don't, I won't go to private school. I know I can't go to the high school. But I'll do something—run away, or go down to Pittsburgh and live with Mom's folks, or something. But I won't go to private school or any of that."

They both looked at me. Then Skipper and Uncle Foster looked at each other. Skipper nodded. "I thought it would be something like that." He laid his cane across his lap. "All right, Christopher, we'll negotiate. Frankie Scalzo is the one you're most concerned about, isn't he?"

"No," I said. "All three."

"Three?" Uncle Foster said.

"Mr. Briggs, too."

Skipper shook his head. "Not him, Christopher. He killed *my* dog. I have to have him."

I felt strange, weird, dealing away these people's lives—kind of cool, with my voice seeming to come from another part of the room. "But Benny, though. Frankie and Benny."

He sat there thinking for a minute. Just for a moment he smiled a tiny smile. "You're going to be a pretty tough negotiator one of these days, Christopher. All right, let's do what you often have to do in these situations. We'll split the difference. I'll take Briggs Senior, you take Scalzo, and we'll let Briggs Junior off with a misdemeanor charge and a year's probation. How does that sit with you?"

That, I knew, was take it or leave it. "You promise."

He suddenly sat up straight and his eyes flashed. "Christopher, never ask me that. If I make a deal, you count on my word for every inch of it."

I blushed. "I'm sorry. I take it back."

Uncle Foster shook his head. "I don't like it, Skipper. If Chris can't get his loyalties straight, that's his problem."

"Give him time, Foster," Skipper said. "He's a good boy, but he needs time." Then he stood up and put out his hand. I took it and we shook. "You can call your girl and put her mind at ease," he said. "But I wouldn't give any details. Just say that the boys won't be going to jail. Perhaps she'll look on you more favorably."

But she wouldn't; I knew that. I would call and tell

168

her that Frankie was safe. Then I would hang up. After that, what would I do? I would go to Wakefield, because that was my part of the bargain, and if they wanted to send me to college, I guess I would do that, too. But would I come into the business the way they expected me to? I had just spent ten minutes trading for people's lives. Was that what you had to do if you wanted power? Did I want to be that way?

I didn't know. "Thank you," I said. Then I went out of the office and down the hall to call Marie.

JAMES LINCOLN COLLIER is a musician as well as the award-winning author of many books for young people. His novels include the Newbery Honor Book *My Brother Sam Is Dead* (with his brother Christopher Collier), *Planet Out of the Past*, *The Teddy Bear Habit*, and *Outside Looking In*. His books on jazz include *Inside Jazz, The Great Jazz Artists*, and *Louis Armstrong*. He lives in New York City.